Guns for the Saratoga

Guns for the Saratoga

STEPHEN W. MEADER

Illustrated by John O'Hara Cosgrave II

SOUTHERN SKIES

ISBN 978-1-931177- 86-3 cloth
ISBN 978-1-931177- 87-0 paperback

Library of Congress Catalog Card Number: 55-8680

LITTLE ROCK, ARKANSAS
www.southernskies.com

Dedication

The republication of this book is dedicated with love to Victor H. Nixon---outstanding minister, trusted advisor, great friend---by Jerry Atchley

FOREWORD

THE FRIENDSHIPS an author makes are often vitally important to the things he writes. Such a friendship is in large part responsible for this book.

I had known William Bell Clark for more than twenty-five years and was well aware of his reputation as the outstanding authority on the American Navy in the Revolution. Then I read his book, *The First Saratoga.* At once I knew that here was the historical material for an adventure novel boys and girls would like.

Bill Clark is retired now, and does his writing in the charming little town of Brevard, North Carolina. But the next time I saw him we talked about my idea for a story. He was both generous and enthusiastic.

I have followed his accurate historical background almost to the letter and it is safe to say no book for young readers about our War for Independence was ever more carefully documented. With only two exceptions, all the members of the *Saratoga's* crew mentioned in my story are real names, taken from the ship's muster rolls. Gideon

Jones and his friend Aaron Mathis are characters of my own invention, but their Mullica River country in South Jersey is real, and little changed today since Revolutionary times. In collections of fine old iron pieces the Batsto mark can still be seen, though the forge itself has long been a crumbling ruin.

I am indebted to Miss Lois Given, of the Historical Society of Pennsylvania for help in some items of research; to Rev. Henry Charlton Beck, whose *Jersey Genesis* is a delightful commentary on the Mullica; and to Dr. Edward N. Murray and his son Ted, who have taken me exploring on that lovely river.

Stephen W. Meader

1955

Guns for the Saratoga

THE BOY GIDEON JONES was a lanky fifteen-year-old in 1777, when he first heard the name "Saratoga." Down where he lived, at the Forks of the Mullica River in South Jersey, the fighting in the upper Hudson Valley seemed a long way off. Gid knew the British regulars were beating Washington's makeshift army most of the time, and he'd heard his father say the outlook for the independence of the colonies was pretty bleak. So it was wonderful news when Burgoyne surrendered at Saratoga.

They had a big celebration at Batsto Furnace. The iron molders and forge men, the teamsters and bog iron diggers —even the charcoal burners—left their jobs and came in to the crossroads store that night. Every patriot for miles around helped build the bonfire, and while they sang and whooped it up for Liberty the mugs of ale and applejack passed from hand to hand.

It wasn't until the next day they discovered that a gang of "refugees"—Tories, deserters and jailbreakers who favored the British side—had seized the chance to burn a barn or two and run off the cattle while they were celebrating. One of the renegades was caught, beaten and thrown in the stout log jail for trial. But everybody knew the ringleader had got away. The raid bore all the earmarks of a Mulliner job. And the outlaw Joe Mulliner was harder to catch than a gray fox. He had his own trails and hideouts, deep in the cedar swamps and spongs.

So the word "Saratoga" was firmly imbedded in Gid's mind. He remembered it through the two years that followed—years when he was filling out and putting on muscle.

The war seemed to come closer to Batsto after that. Colonel Cox organized a company of militia to guard the ironworks, and the men toiled night and day to fill the orders for cannon and shot that kept coming from the Continental Congress.

Cox was a driver. He wasn't much of an expert at making iron, but he left that part of it to Reuben Jones, Gid's father. Meanwhile he rode all over the countryside, hiring woodchoppers and charcoal burners and organizing trains of farmers' wagons to haul the finished guns and ammunition. In the evenings he sat at his great cherry desk and wrote letters to Governor Livingston, General Washington and his many other friends in the patriot cause.

In the winter of 'seventy-seven, while the British held Philadelphia and the patriot army shivered miserably at Valley Forge, Gid kept almost too warm. His father decided he was old enough to go to work and set him to shoveling bog ore, oyster shells and charcoal into the blast furnace. Later, in the following summer, he learned the art of sand molding in the foundry. It was a proud day when he saw his first twelve-pound shot roll into the cooling trough, round and clean and solid.

Batsto was one of half a dozen furnaces and forges scattered through the Jersey Pines. In more peaceful days it had forged bar iron for the blacksmiths of the region. The ore that had been deposited for centuries in the Jersey bogs was purer than any that could be mined. For that reason it withstood rust and was in great demand.

Another kind of activity that brought the war close was the building and outfitting of privateers along the Mullica. The little ships—sloops and schooners and brigs—were manned by fishermen and baymen who knew every gut and channel among the marshy islands at the river's mouth. They would dart out through Little Egg Inlet on an early morning tide, sail twenty or thirty miles to the eastward and harry the coastwise shipping that carried supplies to the British in New York. Hardly a week passed that they failed to bring in prizes. Usually these were small craft, loaded with lumber or vegetables. But once in a while the privateers succeeded in capturing big, armed merchant-men, carrying valuable cargoes of wine and tobacco. When that happened the goods were sold at auction and supplied cash that was sorely needed by the struggling colonies.

Sometimes the daring little ships tackled something too big to handle. In that case they had to scurry for Great Bay under all canvas, with the enemy in hot pursuit. Once they were inside, it was a hopeless chase. Their shallow draft, and the familiarity of their crews with the island passages, enabled them to leave the British cannon far out of range.

Like all the able-bodied youngsters along the river, Gid Jones yearned to sail in the privateers. Some of his friends had received as much as forty or fifty dollars for their share in a single prize. But his father had other ideas.

"Reckon you can do more for General Washingon right here at the ironworks, casting cannon balls. Colonel Cox is building a little fort down at Chestnut Neck, and the guns down there are going to need round shot, in case the redcoats ever get serious about coming up the river."

So the boy continued to sweat over the molten iron all through that hot summer and into the fall.

It was the beginning of October when the British did just what Reuben Jones had predicted. Gid was sitting on a piling beside the river, cooling off in the dusk of the evening, when a man on a lathered horse came galloping down the road from Quaker Bridge. He pulled up beside the wharf and wiped his dusty face.

"Where'll I find Colonel Cox?" he asked huskily.

Gid jumped up. "Come on, I'll show you," he said. " 'Tisn't far." He sprinted ahead past the iron works with the tired horse jogging behind him.

The colonel lived in a big house on a rise of ground, back from the river. Being the manager's son gave Gid certain privileges, and he didn't hesitate to knock at the door. An old black servant opened it and grinned at the boy.

"Yassuh, Marse Gid?" he queried.

"Better fetch the colonel quick, 'Lisha," Gid told him.

"There's a post rider here, an' he must have mighty important news."

At that moment John Cox appeared. He was a stocky, florid-faced man with a determined jut to his chin. The horseman had dismounted and now stood at Gid's elbow. He touched his hat brim.

"I come all the way from Mt. Holly since mornin'," he said. "Committee o' Safety sent me. Looks like Sir Henry Clinton's got his back up an' he's fixin' to clean out everythin' from Great Bay to the Forks. There's a big fleet comin'—mebbe off the inlet right now. I been warnin' the folks along the way, but my hoss is like to founder now."

"Come in," said Cox. "You, 'Lisha, get this man a drink an' have his nag taken care of. By the way," he addressed the messenger again, "are any of our troops on the way?"

"Yeah! Count Pulaski's comin' with his legion. They started 'bout the same time I did but I figger it'll take 'em two days or more to the lower river."

"Gid," said the colonel crisply, "go get Bill Leek and John Cranmer. Tell 'em to saddle the best horses they can find. We've got to get the word down river."

The boy didn't wait to ask any questions. He raced the quarter mile to Leek's house and gave the young militiaman the colonel's message. But John Cranmer had gone off into the pines for firewood and might be late getting back.

Gid had a good mare of his own in the stable at home. He wasted no time, but threw the saddle on her, told his father what was happening, and set off at a gallop down the river road. After a mile or two he overtook Bill Leek and rode along beside him.

"We'd better split up," Bill told him. "You go on to Green Bank an' Lower Bank. I'll cut over to Wading River an' New Gretna an' from there down to the Neck."

At the next fork he waved an arm in farewell and swung his horse to the left, leaving Gid to follow the sandy track along the river. It was getting pretty dark by now, but the mare knew the way and moved ahead at a steady lope. The boy didn't push her. They had a long ride before them and there was no point in tiring her out.

At Green Bank there were two or three houses with lights in the windows. Gid pulled up at the first one and shouted a halloo. When the door opened and a man appeared he gave him the news.

"There's a big fleet coming into the bay," he said. "The word we got is that they're aiming to clean out the whole river. If you've got any prizes moored at the landing you'd better move 'em as far upstream as you can."

Then, while the man still gaped at him, he dug his heels into Blossom's flanks and galloped away. He forded a couple of small creeks and reached Lower Bank, where the same warning was repeated. It was still an hour or two before midnight. Gid decided to keep on all the way to Chestnut Neck, in case anything happened to delay the other messenger.

He stopped several times, at lonely farms and fisher-men's shacks, to spread the alarm. Then, in the pitch dark of a moonless night, he reached the banks of the Wading. At this point, near where it joined the bigger Mullica, the stream was misnamed. It was tide water and deep. He put the mare cautiously down the bank and gave her her head. She lunged into the water and struck out gallantly for the farther shore. In a minute or two her feet touched bottom and she scrambled up to dry ground, shaking herself like a dog.

There wasn't much of a road here along the lower river. The houses were built close to the shore and most people traveled by boat when they wanted to go anywhere. As he rode along Gid could make out the spars of brigs and schooners, moored in the channel. He thought there must be a dozen captured vessels in that reach of water, besides the privateer craft.

He gave his warning at several houses, asking the sleepy people to spread the word among their neighbors. Then, as he neared the earthworks of the little fort, a sentry challenged him.

"Who be ye, an' what d' ye want?" the gruff voice asked. "Don't come any closer or I'll fire."

"Message from Colonel Cox," the boy replied. "I'm Gid Jones, from Batsto Forge. Where's your officer?"

"Home in bed," said the man. "I'm just here to watch the guns."

"Well," Gid told him, "we'd better get the garrison here before long or the British'll have the fort, guns an' all."

Someone in the village above must have waked the lieutenant in charge of the fort. He appeared at a run, fumbling with the buckle of his sword, his clothes still in disarray. It was too dark for Gid to see his face, but as soon as the man spoke he knew he was a bayman turned soldier.

"Where be they?" the lieutenant asked. "Somebody say the fleet's been sighted?"

"We got the word up at Batsto," Gid explained. "Colonel Cox sent two of us to warn the river folks. Here comes Bill Leek now."

The other messenger rode up at that moment and confirmed the boy's story. "You better get your men together an' look to the primin' of your cannon," he told the lieutenant. "Got enough powder an' shot?"

" 'Nough to make it hot for 'em," the militia officer nodded. "Won't last long, but we'll do our best. What about you fellers—goin' to stay here an' help us fight?"

Gid was tempted, but Leek decided against it. "If they get by you here at the Neck," he said, "we've got to be up river to protect the ironworks. 'Bout all we can do is wish you luck."

They rested the horses for an hour and ate some bread and cheese with the men of the garrison. Then they started the return journey. There was no longer any reason for hurry. After they crossed the Wading River, they let their mounts choose their own pace, and it was early dawn when they rode into Batsto.

Gid's father told him to sleep through the morning. There would be no work at the foundry that day. The colonel had called on every farmer in the neighborhood to bring teams and wagons, and loads of cannon balls were already moving off into the woods to be hidden.

When the boy woke up there was a tramp of many feet

in the street outside. Going to the window he saw the militia company drawn up in ragged formation and heard the sergeants bawling commands. Before Gid was dressed the troop marched off southward.

That afternoon and evening were filled with excitement. Toward dusk they heard the dull boom of distant cannonading. Later a rider came up the river with news of disaster. The British had left their big ships in the bay and rowed in with oared galleys that carried heavy guns. The little fort had given a good account of itself, but within half an hour the earthworks had been smashed and the cannon put out of commission. The garrison had given up and run back into the woods.

After that, the messenger said, the lobsterbacks really went to work. There must have been several hundred trained soldiers in the attacking party, and they burned or took away the shipping, blew up the sheds where prize goods were stored, fired a dozen houses in the village and slaughtered the stock. The rider hadn't waited to see any more, but it seemed likely that the victorious redcoats would continue up the river.

Colonel Cox looked grim, his jaw jutting out farther than ever. "By thunder," he growled, "they'll run into a hornets' nest if they get much closer. We've got men posted at every turn of the river, where they can rake those galleys from stem to stern. Besides, Pulaski ought to be down here by now. He may not have any artillery, but he's got enough good troops to give 'em what-for."

Nobody slept much that night. At daybreak Gid and his father loaded muskets and went to the wooded point below the forge, where breastworks had been thrown up. Everything movable had been carried off for safekeeping and the women and children were in farmhouses miles away.

All day the militiamen lay in their positions behind the barricade, fighting mosquitoes and waiting. Just before dark a scout rode in from down river. Wearily he swung off his horse and reported to the colonel.

"Reckon it's all over," he said. "One o' the galleys grounded on a bar an' the Britishers figgered the river was too shallow. Anyhow they've gone back to the fleet."

In their relief, the garrison let out a cheer and the colonel allowed them to tap a barrel of ale. Soon they were straggling back to their deserted houses and sending wagons to collect their families. It wasn't until three days later that the people of Batsto heard the final story of the affair.

Two men in a sailing skiff came up the river and tied up to the wharf. They were elderly baymen from Chestnut Neck.

"There's been a turr'ble massacre," was all they would say at first. Under Colonel Cox's urging they came out with the rest of the story.

It seemed Count Pulaski's Legion had finally arrived at Tuckerton, commonly known as Middle-of-the-Shore. He marched on down through the marshes till he could watch the British trying to free two of their ships from a sandbar in the harbor. That night he threw out a picket post of about fifty men under Baron de Bosen, who camped at a farmhouse on the Island Road. A spy got word to Captain Ferguson, in command of the British landing force, and about midnight his men crept up through the brush.

They overpowered a sleepy sentry, then moved on to take the whole picket force by surprise. More than forty of them, including Baron de Bosen, were slaughtered in cold blood, and the raiders got clean away before Pulaski could retaliate.

The massacre at Chestnut Neck was one of the blackest chapters in the war, and it made an impression on young Gid Jones that he would never forget.

FOR A MONTH or two the people of the Mullica were so busy rebuilding their homes and getting in such harvests as had been spared that nobody had time to think much about privateering. By early December, however, the burned-out families had some sort of roofs over their heads and kindly neighbors saw to it that they were fed.

A few fast sailing craft remained and the yards were hard at work building new ones. One of the older ships, undamaged by the British raid, was the schooner *Rattlesnake*, which had been moored at Green Bank. She was armed with half a dozen six-pounder guns and carried a good spread of canvas. Because of her shallow draft, she couldn't sail too close to the wind, but was fast before the wind and able to thread the channels of the bay islands.

In January her skipper, Captain William Treen, took the schooner down to an anchorage off Deep Point in the upper bay. No ice had formed on the Mullica up to that time, and he wanted her in salt water before she was frozen in.

A day or two later an acquaintance of Gid's, young Aaron Mathis, came to Batsto and looked the boy up at the foundry. He was a broad-shouldered lad of twenty and had sailed in privateers for three or four years.

"Gid," he announced proudly, "I'm goin' as mate o' the *Rattlesnake!* Cap'n Treen figgers the British have got careless since October. Ought to be some fat pickin's if they think all the privateers were wiped out. How 'bout sailin' with us next week?"

"I'd sure like to," Gid told him. "Maybe Dad'll let me go this time. I'll ask him, anyhow. Why don't you come home with me an' have supper with us?"

Aaron accepted the invitation. When the meal was finished, and the men were sitting by the fire, Gid brought up the subject of the privateer's cruise. To his surprise his father didn't veto the idea of his going.

"Might do you good to learn a little seamanship," he said. "And after that raid last fall I'd like to see the British take a licking or two. Your ma won't think much of the idea, but I guess I can keep her from worrying."

Aaron grinned and shook Gid's hand. "See you down at Deep Point next Tuesday," he said, "an' I'll get you signed on. Bring along your warmest underclothes an' wool stockin's, an' a good, thick jacket if you've got one. These winter cruises can be almighty cold."

Gid was given a lift down river in an oyster boat four days later. He had to leave home at two in the morning, his clothes and necessaries snugly packed in a canvas sea bag. The temperature was close to freezing and a sharp night wind blew from the north. He was shivering, even in his wool jersey and heavy jacket.

With a favoring tide and a breeze on the port quarter, the sailing skiff made good time, and it was only an hour after sunrise when they reached the mile-wide water of the upper bay. The schooner was moored alongside a make-shift pier on Deep Point.

Gid went ashore, thrashing his arms for warmth, and was greeted by the young mate. In the schooner's cabin, a few minutes later, he was introduced to Captain Treen. The skipper was a small, wiry man, quick in his move-ments. He gave the boy's hand a hard grip and looked him in the eye.

"This is no picnic we're goin' on, Jones," he snapped. "If you've never been to sea before, there'll be times you'll wish you hadn't. You'll be wet an' cold an' you may get shot to glory. If you still want to come, sign your name here."

*   *   *

In the course of the next three weeks Gid had occasion to remember those words only too well. The *Rattlesnake* pitched and rolled in the rough winter seas and for two days he was miserably seasick. He never seemed to get enough sleep, for sick or not he had to turn up with the watch every four hours. And the coarse food—salt pork, potatoes, fish-head chowder and ship's biscuit—made him retch whenever he looked at it.

On the third day the nausea left him and he staggered on deck, weak and pale, to find the sun shining and the ship running southward on an even keel. He ate breakfast and kept it down. By noon he was feeling so much better that he really began to learn something about his job.

As the only green hand among the crew of thirty men, he received more attention than would ordinarily be given a beginner. Mathis, the bosun and the gunner's mate all took turns instructing him. As a consequence he soon became familiar with the rig of the vessel. In a week's time he could do a fair job at the wheel, reef a topsail and run up the ratlines almost as fast as the other sailors.

He learned what it meant to stand watch. And though there wasn't enough ammunition to waste on target practice, he got some instruction in serving the six-pounder guns, carrying powder and shot, and handling the buckets if fire should break out.

Discipline aboard the privateer was a free and easy business. The officers and crew were all neighbors ashore, so there was little need for the rope's end. They took orders good-naturedly, fished when they felt like it, traded watches and settled occasional squabbles with their fists. While all of them were more or less in favor of the patriot cause, they had shipped for what they could get out of the voyage for themselves.

Twice in the first week they sighted sails, but each time they found the merchant vessels were in convoy, escorted by warships of the Royal Navy. The second time it happened, the *Rattlesnake* was sighted and had to take to her heels. After a chase of a dozen miles night hid her from the pursuing frigate, and when morning came she was alone again in the gray sea.

They had been cruising offshore between Sandy Hook and the Delaware Capes for sixteen days and the crew had begun to grumble when the lookout raised a lone sail to starboard. Captain Treen ordered all canvas set and the men snapped to it with alacrity.

The other vessel was a little two-masted snow, hurrying northward before the wind. Close-hauled, the schooner lay over in a long reach that would cut across the bows of the smaller craft. Up to that time the privateer had been flying no colors. Now Aaron Mathis ran up a tattered old flag. It wasn't the new Stars and Stripes but the rattlesnake flag, from which the schooner took her name. Crudely sewn on the bunting was a coiled snake and the inscription "Don't tread on me."

"It fools 'em sometimes," the mate told Gid with a grin. "They can't figger what country's flag it is till we're right on top of 'em."

The starboard guns had been loaded meanwhile, and the gunners stood ready to light their slow-matches. After their own fashion the crew had cleared the deck for action. Gid's post was by the big cask, filled with sea water, that stood at the foremast foot. He had two wooden buckets ready in case of fire.

The schooner swept down fast, closing the gap between her and her prey. They could make out tiny figures aboard the snow now, and see them scurrying about the deck like agitated ants. Gid had a chilly feeling at the pit of his stomach. He was going into battle for the first time.

"How many guns d' ye see?" called the captain to the lookout.

"Two swivels," the seaman answered. "Fore an' aft. They're loadin' the stern gun now."

A moment later Gid saw a puff of smoke and then a round shot screamed past, twenty yards off the schooner's starboard bow.

"They're in range," the gunner's mate grunted. "Aim ain't so good, though."

Captain Treen held his course, rapidly narrowing the distance while the snow's crew reloaded in frantic haste. Their next shot was high but true. It tore a rent in the privateer's fore topsail without damaging the mast or cordage.

The vessels were less than a cable's length apart now, and the *Rattlesnake's* guns were trained for point-blank range.

"Heave to!" roared Treen. "Surrender or I'll give you a broadside!"

All the fight went out of the snow's crew as they looked into the menacing muzzles of the cannon. A white piece of cloth was waved and the British flag was hastily hauled down.

Both ships swung into the wind and the mate boarded the prize with an armed boat's crew. They were within easy hailing distance. Gid saw the men aboard the snow disarmed while Mathis held a brief conference with the captured craft's skipper.

"She's the *Molly B,* out o' Nassau," he reported. "Light cargo—mostly sugar an' tobacco."

"Send two men back with the boat," Treen answered. "Then take her in. We'll follow. Accordin' to my reckonin' we're off Cape May, so you've got a fair wind."

They tied up with their prize at Chestnut Neck early the next morning and all hands got a week's leave ashore. The snow and her cargo were worth two or three thousand dollars in hard money, so the crew of the *Rattlesnake* felt like celebrating. Gid slept in his own bed that night, and found it strangely quiet after the tossing of his bunk in the fo'c's'le. He was fast becoming a seasoned old salt.

His mother did her best to spoil him that week. She insisted that he sleep as late as he liked in the mornings and fed him all his favorite dishes. When it was time for him to go back to the schooner she wept a little.

On her second cruise the *Rattlesnake* was less fortunate. South, off the Maryland coast, she ran into a winter storm that battered her for three long days. Desperately the crew clung to the icy rigging and handlines as they clawed their way out to sea. Once they were blown so far to leeward that they could see the line of surf on the beach through the flying scud.

After the weather cleared and the storm damage was repaired, they voyaged northward again, looking for coast-wise shipping. Two fruitless weeks went by before they sighted a sail. Then, off Barnegat, they overtook a big, slow-moving brig. She was flying the British flag but appeared to be unarmed.

Captain Treen sent a shot across her bows and she promptly hove to. In answer to the privateer's hail her commander identified her as the *Miranda*, out of Halifax, with a cargo of salt cod and lumber. After a few threats from Treen her flag was hauled down in token of surrender.

Jubilant, they sent the bosun with twelve men in the cutter to board her and sail her in. Gid saw the prize crew pull alongside and start to climb over the bulwarks. Then suddenly the rail was swarming with seamen. They swung their cutlasses with devastating effect, cutting down some of the Americans and forcing others to drop into the sea. At the same moment concealed gunports in the brig's side were flung open and the schooner's men were staring into the ugly mouths of cannon.

Treen acted fast. "Let go sheets," he yelled. "Helm hard over!"

The privateer fell off quickly before the wind and cut past the brig's bow. It was done in the nick of time, for the first broadside missed the *Rattlesnake's* stern by inches.

The British flag was back at the main truck of the brig now, and her men were putting on all the canvas she would carry. There was no possibility of picking up the boat's crew. The schooner had to flee for her life. Luckily there was a good breeze. Before the larger craft could maneuver into position for another broadside she was out of range.

It was a long-faced crowd of privateersmen that crossed the bar into Great Bay that night. Four of their comrades were probably drowned and eight or nine others wounded or captured. Almost equally galling was the fact that they had been outsmarted by the enemy. For two days the *Miranda* cruised outside, daring them to come out. Then she sailed off to the southward.

Captain Treen was not a man to brood long over a defeat. Within a couple of weeks he had recruited a few additional hands, provisioned the ship, and was ready for sea again. In the face of some objection from his father, Gid was resolved to make one more voyage. He went aboard the last day of February and they sailed next day.

Some of the new men were even greener than he had been. He watched their sufferings with sympathy and when they got over their seasickness he helped teach them the ropes. Grimes, the new bosun, was a surly fellow, never well liked by others in the crew. Now that he had some authority he bullied the landlubbers unmercifully.

One night when Gid was on watch he heard the bosun's

snarling voice and saw him lumbering toward the scuttle-butt. A raw youngster by the name of Cummins had gone there for a drink of water.

"Look'ee here," the petty officer growled. "I sent ye forrard to keep watch. Wotcher doin' here?"

"I was just thirsty," Cummins pleaded. "Can't a feller get a drink o' water?"

That was all the excuse Grimes needed. "None o' yer lip!" he muttered. And with that he clouted the boy on the ear, knocking him into the scuppers.

Gid's temper flared. "You'd no call to do that!" he told the bosun. "What's wrong with getting a drink?"

With an oath Grimes lunged forward, swinging his fists. Gid ducked the first wild blow and sidestepped the second. Then, with the bosun still advancing, he drove his own right to the pit of the older man's stomach. Grimes staggered backward and sat down heavily on the deck.

Before the fight could go any farther, Aaron Mathis came forward from the afterdeck at a run. Angrily he sent Gid to the foretop and told the bosun to get below.

That ended the affair, but for the rest of the voyage Gid was careful to keep out of Grimes' way. He knew the young mate sympathized with him. Still, striking a petty officer, even in self defense, was hardly excusable.

Four days later, on the eighth of March, they sighted a sail a few miles below Sandy Hook. The craft turned out to be a broad-beamed Dutch sloop carrying what looked like a deckload of hay.

"Hardly worth takin'," Captain Treen grumbled. "Still,

she's out o' Staten Island, in British-held waters, so she's a fair enough prize."

The *Rattlesnake* approached with more caution this time, her guns loaded and run out in case of trouble. In answer to Treen's hail, the skipper replied in broken English. They were poor Dutch farmers, he said, and all they had aboard was some hay and a few vegetables that they hoped to sell in the Delaware.

There was very little sea running and the schooner was able to come close alongside. Treen was still prepared for a trick.

"Jones," he ordered, "take five men an' board her. See if they're tellin' the truth. We'll keep you covered if they start any ruckus."

Gid crossed the rail, cutlass in hand, and faced the captain and four sullen seamen. They offered no resistance, and a glance around told him there were no cannon hidden.

"Hold 'em there by the wheel," he told his men. "I'll just check up on this cargo."

The Dutch skipper started to expostulate, but Gid paid no attention. With the point of his sword he probed deep into the hay. For a while he felt nothing. Then the cutlass clinked against metal. Reaching down to the full length of his arm he searched about until his hand gripped the barrel of a musket. There were others beside it—row upon row of them.

He stood up, brushing the hay off his sleeve. "Better tie those folks up," he told his boarding party.

It was obvious to the schooner's crew that Gid had found something more important than hay. They waited impatiently while he cut one of the ropes that bound the load and began pitching armfuls of the loose hay aside. Finally he stood up, grinning.

"What is it?" Treen called. "What did ye find?"

"Fifty British muskets," the boy replied proudly. "All new guns with the king's mark on the stocks."

He went aft and faced the Dutch skipper. "Where were you taking 'em?" he asked threateningly.

The other man shook his head and held out his hands, pretending not to understand.

"Search him," Gid ordered, and two of the privateersmen proceeded to go through his pockets. After a moment a piece of folded paper was extracted from inside the captain's shirt.

Gid opened it and read the message. It was addressed to "J. Molyneaux, Esq., at ye Forks of Tuckyhaw River, Province of West Jersey."

Below was written: "This cargo of fodder compleats ye goods consigned to you. Ye bearer, Mynheer Verplanck, is trustworthy and will return any messages you may have for His Majesty's forces at New York."

It was signed by a "Maj. Jno. Esterly, Adjt."

Gid scrambled up the schooner's side and handed the note to Captain Treen. Not a very well educated man, the skipper read it with difficulty.

"Who the devil is this J. Molly-what's-his-name?" he asked.

"I figure it must be a Tory," Gid answered. "And there's only one Tory I know of with a name anything like that —Joe Mulliner."

"Mulliner!" the captain exclaimed. "Sure as shootin'! So that's where he's hidin' now—over on the Tuckahoe. Colonel Cox'll be glad to know that."

He slapped Gid on the back. "She's your prize, boy. Think you can sail her in?"

"Aye, aye, sir," Gid replied, beaming. "It'll be easier if you take the prisoners aboard here, though."

Ten minutes later the *Rattlesnake* bore off and the young prize-master was on his own. Fortunately he had some experienced sailors in his crew. They trimmed the broad mainsail, set both jibs to catch the light westerly breeze, and the sloop went lumbering southward.

There was always danger that a cruising corvette out of New York might overtake them, and Gid kept a sharp eye on the horizon astern. The schooner was hull down to the east and had shortened sail to keep pace with the slower vessel. All night the breeze held and the sloop passed

Barnegat Inlet at dawn. Off Tucker Island they waited for high tide, then crossed the bar and tacked up the channel into Great Bay in the early afternoon.

It was nearly suppertime the next day when Gid reached Batsto. He had brought the sloop up river as far as Green Bank and left her there under guard. Now he went directly to Colonel Cox's mansion. The Negro, Elisha, met him at the door with a grin.

"Cunnel's busy right now," he told the boy, "but ah reckon he'll see you. Ah'll tell him you're here."

"Thanks," said Gid. "I've got some news for him."

After a few minutes Cox came from his study and shook the boy's hand. "How'd the privateering go?" he asked genially.

Gid told him in a few words about the last cruise, and the capture of the British muskets. Then he pulled the folded note out of his pocket.

"The Dutchman was carrying this," he said.

The colonel read it quickly and returned to the name at the top with a frown. "Molyneaux," he murmured. "Say, isn't that the way Joe Mulliner's folks used to spell it? By thunder, boy, this is worth getting! There's a militia company at May's Landing, over on the Great Egg River. The Forks o' the Tuckahoe wouldn't be more'n four or five leagues south o' there. I'll send a rider tonight—see if we can surprise that murdering devil!"

When he got home, the boy found news of the prize had preceded him. His mother welcomed him with open arms and hurried a big supper on the table. His father, too, was glad to see him, but he looked tired and worn.

"We're short of men at the works," he explained. "More and more orders come in from the Congress, and we have to keep going day and night. I stay there till midnight most o' the time."

Gid was concerned. "Gosh, Dad," he said, "I didn't know it was that bad. I'm through with sailoring for a spell anyhow, an' I'll go back to work in the morning."

The words seemed to please his father. "Good," he smiled. "We sure can use you at the foundry."

That was in March, 1779. The war dragged on, now well into its third year, and still the patriots had little to cheer about. True, the British had abandoned Philadelphia and the Continental Congress was in session there. But the area around New York was firmly held by Clinton's regulars, and now a big new attack was being launched in the South, with Georgia and South Carolina apparently in the hands of the redcoats.

What made things worse was the lack of real money. Continental paper money was plentiful, but would buy so little that it was a joke. "Not worth a Continental" had become a common expression. At Batsto Forge the iron-workers who had once been happy to earn a dollar a day now received forty dollars in paper and grumbled at their wages. Only the farmers and the privateers were sure of getting enough to eat.

There were still many Loyalist sympathizers in that part of Jersey. Most of them were quiet, peaceful people and were left alone. There was a rougher element, however, that had given the Tories a bad name. Such men, joining forces with "refugees" like Mulliner, were a real menace. Whenever a chance offered they came out of the woods to rob, plunder and burn, and they furnished spies to guide the British raids.

After two or three days word came back from May's Landing that the militia had marched south after the Tory leader. Then, at the end of a week, Gid heard they had returned, empty-handed. From a scared boy at the Forks of the Tuckahoe they had learned that Mulliner and his men had left the night before—gone into hiding somewhere deep in the cedar swamps.

All through that grim year Gid worked hard at the foundry. Scattered and weak as Washington's forces were, the spirit of resistance was as strong as ever. The Continental troops who had been in it from the beginning had hardened into tough, determined fighters, able to hold their own against any soldiers in the world. But to be effective they needed guns, powder and shot. Supplies of powder had been brought by the French fleet. But for the rest they had to depend on the output of little iron forges and foundries like the one at Batsto.

The following spring Gid celebrated his eighteenth birthday. He was a big lad now, six feet tall and powerfully built. Handling pig iron had developed his arms and shoulders.

One evening in early April Aaron Mathis came to see him. More than once the boy had wished he could be back at sea with the privateers, and talking to the mate of the *Rattlesnake* strengthened that feeling.

"Got a berth open for you aboard the schooner," Aaron

told him with a grin. "We'll be sailin' in a week. I guess you heard about the latest prize. We took a big armed sloop called the *Speedwell*. Mighty fine cargo, too. 'Baccy, sugar, coffee an' china—close to five thousand dollars' worth. My share ought to be 'round three hundred in gold. I bet you don't make that sort o' money here."

Gid shook his head ruefully. "I haven't seen any gold or silver for a year," he said. "I'd sure like to sail with you. Soon as Dad gets home I'll talk it over with him."

Reuben Jones came up the road at that moment. There were wrinkles in his forehead and he looked worried. At the door he shook hands with Mathis, started to go inside, then turned again to the privateer mate.

"Do you know any men down river who'd be willing to come up here and work a couple o' months?" he asked. "We're short-handed and just got a big order. Sixteen double reinforced nine-pounders. The Navy's building a new sloop-of-war up at Philadelphia, and the guns are for her. She's called the *Saratoga*."

Gid's hopes took a tumble. "I guess that settles my plans," he told Mathis. "You'll have to sail without me —unless you'd like to lay over a voyage an' help cast those cannon!"

The stocky young mate rubbed his jaw thoughtfully. Then he looked up and grinned. "By cracky," he exclaimed, "I'll do that! I been a little ashamed o' what I been doin' for the country. Guns for the Continental Navy sounds like somethin' worth while."

*   *   *

The name of the new naval vessel had stirred Gid's memory, recalled the jubilation of that first big American victory at Saratoga. With Aaron at his side he labored harder than ever to get the guns ready in time for delivery on the promised date—the tenth of June.

Sweating over the huge molds, or watching the drop-hammers forge the heavy wrought iron bands that reinforced the guns at breach and muzzle, Gid often thought about the sloop-of-war. To carry that much armament she must be of fair size. He knew that "sloop," as applied to a war vessel, didn't mean a single mast and fore-and-aft rig. The craft could be anything from a schooner to a barkentine or a brig—often a small full-rigged ship. Working on her guns gave him a special interest in this particular sloop-of-war and he hoped someday to see her.

By the end of May the casting of the cannon was finished. They were made of good iron, clean and strong. Gid tested every bore for size and found it true. These guns would fire straight.

The forging went more slowly for water was low in the river and the mill wheel that drove the hammers was often idle. Cox raged and fumed at the delay but there was little he could do. Finally, in the first week of June, thunderstorms brought two days of heavy rain. The river rose behind the dam and the big wheel turned steadily.

When the end of the job was in sight, Gid's father prepared to leave for Philadelphia. He would have to arrange for barges at Cooper's Ferry, to get the guns across the Delaware. Meanwhile Gid and Aaron were entrusted with the job of rounding up heavy wagons and teams to pull them.

Reuben Jones rode northward on the eighth of June, still hopeful that he could deliver the cannon two days later.

"I'll meet you at the Bull and Stars," he told Gid. "Colonel Cox has agreed to have you bring up the wagons, and he's furnishing a squad of militia for a guard. I'll be waiting at the inn, two nights from now."

The four big wagons were ready the next morning, and a crew of ironworkers loaded the cannon, four of them to a wagon. In spite of their utmost efforts the boys had been able to gather only a dozen horses. Four-horse teams were necessary to pull through the deep sand, and finally, in desperation, Gid requisitioned two yoke of oxen to fill out the quota.

They got under way before noon, Aaron riding ahead with four militiamen and Gid bringing up the rear with a similar number. From the start the oxen slowed their progress. The big beasts were strong and willing but no amount of goading could make them move much faster than two miles an hour.

In a direct line it was hardly more than thirty miles from Batsto to the Delaware. By the sand roads through the pines the distance was some ten miles farther. Gid's original plan had been to reach the village of Long-a-Coming at the end of the first day. At sunset, however, they were still several miles short of their goal. They came to a log bridge over a stream and Gid rode ahead to confer with Aaron.

"We've got good water here," he said, "an' a fair place to camp. If we kept on it'd be dark before we went far. With an early enough start tomorrow we ought to make it to Cooper's Ferry."

Young Mathis looked around into the deepening dusk of the woods and agreed reluctantly. "I'm willin' to stop here," he said, "but we'd better stand guard. I reckon there's folks would like to stop a shipment like this."

Aaron and his militiamen took the first watch. The teams had been watered, fed and tied beside the wagons, and the men had had a sketchy supper of bread and cheese.

Gid had trouble getting to sleep. It was hot and the mosquitoes swarmed thickly around their camp. Like most Jerseymen his skin was toughened so that he hardly felt the bites, but the humming kept him awake.

Finally he dozed off and it seemed only a moment before his friend was shaking his shoulder. "It's midnight," said Aaron. "I've woke up the rest o' the men. Here—better take these pistols. They're loaded an' primed."

Gid rubbed his eyes, stretched and got up. Going to the brook, he doused his face with cold water, then stuck the pistols carefully in his belt. The moon was past the full but it gave enough light to outline the pines and the crude bridge. Quietly Gid gave orders to his four guards. They weren't a very soldierly group in their homespun clothes, but they had muskets and knew how to shoot them. He posted one at each corner of the little clearing by the road.

A pair of whippoorwills were calling somewhere in the woods close by. Gid stood leaning against one of the wagons, wide awake now, and listening to the noises of the night. His thoughts were on the journey they must make tomorrow.

When the noise of the whippoorwills stopped, the sudden silence was ominous. Gid didn't move from where he stood, but his hands went quietly to the pistol butts. Then an owl hooted softly and an answering hoot came from the opposite side of the clearing. There was something about those calls that didn't sound quite right. Gid drew his pistols. And as he did so the crashing report of a musket came from somewhere near the bridge.

THE YOUNG MILITIAMAN who had been closest to the bridge hurried toward the wagons at a stumbling run. He was trying to reload his gun as he came. Behind him Gid could see half a dozen leaping figures. And as they charged the camp they began yelling.

"George and England! . . . God save the King! . . . Kill the rebels!" they roared.

Gid hurdled the wagon tongue and leveled his pistols. "Halt!" he shouted, and when they came on he took quick aim at the leader and fired. The man toppled forward on his face, a scant five yards away.

For a moment the attackers hesitated. One of them fired at Gid but the musket ball hit the barrel of a cannon on the wagon and glanced off in a whining ricochet. Meanwhile Aaron and his men had been roused by the sentry's shot and the whooping of the Tory band.

"Guard the other side!" Gid shouted. "We'll stand 'em off here."

Hardly had he spoken when more yells arose in the

woods behind them. The horses were rearing and snorting in fear and now the party that had attacked from the bridge gathered fresh courage and came on once more. For a moment it looked as if the little defending group would be thrown into a panic.

But Gid had underestimated the steadiness of the patriot militia. The sentries had fallen back to the shelter of the wagons and now they were loading and firing methodically, making their shots count. The Tories faltered again as two of their number went down. One, bolder than the rest, rushed right into the camp, but Aaron clubbed his empty musket and bashed his head with the butt.

After that the marauders took to their heels. They left one man dead and two wounded in the clearing. Gid called the roll and found all of their own little squad able to answer. The only casualty was a militiaman who had been nicked in the shoulder by a grazing shot.

In the darkness they bound up the wounds as best they could. The two prisoners were tied and put in one of the wagons, along with the body of the slain Tory. Gid was sure he recognized the dead man as one of Joe Mulliner's gang. The other two refused to talk.

Aaron and his four men got a few hours' sleep before dawn, while Gid's sentries continued to stand watch. When the first gray light came, Gid roused them out. He figured they still had twenty-five miles to cover and they needed all the daylight they could get.

When they had been on the road two or three hours they reached the tavern at Long-a-Coming and had a decent breakfast. Then they pushed ahead, resting the horses often to let the ox-team catch up. They were in more settled country now. The road was wider and firmer, and other travelers passed, staring at the iron guns and the bloody bandages.

At Haddonfield, in the afternoon, they turned their prisoners over to the local peace officers. Then Gid rode on in advance of the wagons to keep his appointment with his father. It was seven in the evening when he dismounted from his mare in the courtyard of the Bull and Stars.

Reuben Jones had been waiting in the main room of the inn and hurried out to greet his son.

"You look fair tuckered out, boy," he said with concern. "What's happened? Where are the guns?"

Red-eyed from lack of sleep and stained with dust and sweat, Gid knew he must present a sorry appearance. He grinned wearily and told his father about the night's happenings.

"But we saved the cannon," he finished. "They'll be here by dark, if those blamed oxen'll just keep moving."

Sure enough, by the time Gid had changed his clothes, bathed and eaten supper, the caravan of wagons came plodding up the road from Clements' Bridge.

The inn was only a few hundred yards from the river and after the teams were stabled and the rest of the party fed, Gid and his father walked down the dark lane to the wharves. A mile away, across the black expanse of water, a few lights twinkled.

"That's Philadelphia yonder," said Reuben Jones. "I've hired two barges to carry the guns across. The sloop-of-war's moored down at the Southwark yards where she was built."

Gid had been in the big city only once, years before the war started. Now he stared across, wondering if any of those lights were in the State House, where the Continental Congress met.

"Better get to bed now," his father told him. "I reckon you need sleep after last night, and we'll be up early. Have to unload those cannon and let Mathis take the wagons back."

The next morning dawned hot and clear. After an early breakfast they took the wagons down to the wharf and shipped the guns aboard the barges. They were clumsy, square-ended scows, propelled by four oars on a side.

Gid and his father said good-bye to the other Mullica men and each of them got into one of the barges to watch over their precious cargo. The rowers were a queerly assorted lot. One of Gid's crew had a peg leg and the rest looked like scarecrows, dirty, half-naked and bleary-eyed. Most able-bodied men had left the waterfront long before to fight in the army, serve voluntarily in privateers or as pressed seamen aboard naval vessels. These were the scum that had been left.

He watched them pull half-heartedly at the sweeps and wondered if they would make it across the river. The tide was running out toward the bay. By steering straight across, the drift of the current would carry the barges toward their destination in Southwark.

Gid could see the *Saratoga* clearly now. Her black-painted hull stood out new and gleaming among the nondescript shipping moored along the lower docks. She was ship-rigged, with tall white masts and taut stays. Not a very big craft, he realized—perhaps 150 tons—but trim and businesslike. She looked as if she could move fast.

Twenty minutes later both the barges were nearly alongside, under the ship's starboard rail. A man in a dark blue brass-buttoned coat and cocked hat looked down at them, a sudden grin on his weather-tanned face.

"Guns for the *Saratoga?*" he called. "Well, thank Heaven—one thing that's delivered on time!"

Then the grin vanished. "Hey you—belay and stand off!" he bellowed. "Don't you dare bump the side till I've got fenders over."

He disappeared for a moment, then came hurrying back to drop mats of braided rope down from the rail. When four of them were in place, Reuben Jones ordered the oars in, and the two barges drifted gently in against the fenders.

He looked up at the officer on deck. "My orders," he said, "are to deliver these guns to Captain John Young. Are you Cap'n Young?"

"You've come to the right port of call," the blue-coated man replied, smiling once more. "That's my name. And yours, sir?"

"Reuben Jones, ironmaster, from Batsto. Soon as we can get this cargo aboard, I've got a letter for you from Colonel Cox."

"Fine!" said the captain. "Sorry I've no crew yet, but perhaps your bargemen will give a hand. Five dollars, continental, to every man who wants to earn it. I'll pay out of my own pocket."

The rowers, who had been looking surly at the suggestion of more work, sprang up with alacrity. Under the captain's guidance they rigged shears with a pair of spars and soon swayed the cannon up, one at a time. When they were paid off and gone, Young invited the two Jerseymen down to his cabin.

"We've had endless delays," he told them. "The Congress is so infernally hard up, it's like pulling teeth to get the money for outfitting. I've had to hold off signing a crew till we have hard cash to pay a bonus. Nobody'll ship with the Navy unless we can pay in specie."

While Young read Colonel Cox's note, Gid had an opportunity to stare about him at the snug cabin. It was small but comfortably appointed, infinitely neater than the skipper's quarters aboard the *Rattlesnake*.

Captain Young folded the letter and glanced toward the boy. Gid liked his face. It was strong and square-jawed and there was a lively light in the gray eyes. He looked like a man of action and decision.

"I've no means of entertaining you properly aboard here, gentlemen," he told them. "But my house is on Laurel Street, not far from here. Let's go there for dinner."

Gid's father accepted the invitation and they mounted the companion. There was a big seaman sitting on a coil of cable when they reached the deck. He dropped the line he was splicing and stood up, touching his forelock.

"Any orders for me, sir?" he asked.

"Yes, Patrick. The guns have come aboard, as you see. Guard 'em carefully. When Henderson comes, have him report to Mr. Lewis of the Board of Admiralty that we've got our cannon."

As they went down the gangplank he chuckled. "That's Pat Green," he said. "One man I can depend on. He served with me in the *Impertinent* and gave up a mate's berth in a privateer to sign on as the first able seaman of the *Saratoga*."

In a few minutes they were climbing the marble steps of a two-story brick house. It was a pleasant-looking place, well kept, with fresh lace curtains at the windows.

"Joanna!" called the captain as he opened the door, and immediately Mistress Young appeared in the hall. She was a plump and pretty woman in her frilly white cap and brown bombazine gown.

"Guests for dinner, my dear," said John Young, and made the introductions.

The lady curtsied, ushered them into the living room, and went to the rear of the house where they could hear her giving orders to the cook.

Gid's father made a polite comment about the new sloop-of-war and asked when she would be ready for sea.

At once the captain's eyes lit up. This was a subject close to his heart.

"She's ready now," he said, "except for building gun carriages, provisioning and signing a crew. I've got my officers picked, right down to the midshipmen. Some Jerseymen among 'em, by the way. Young Jack Livingston, the son of your Governor Livingston, is coming as a mid-shipman.

"As to seamen, we should have no trouble as soon as there's hard cash to pay 'em. I'm told there's a good cargo of wine from a prize to be sold soon, and if Francis Lewis has his way, we'll get the proceeds to hire a crew."

"The ship looks fast," Reuben Jones put in. "Nice lines."

The captain grinned. "Mr. Humphreys, the master builder, says she'll outsail anything in the British fleet," he replied proudly. "How she'll fight is another matter. That'll be my responsibility."

He went on enthusiastically describing his new ship for another half hour. Then a little Negro boy in a bright green jacket came to the door, bowed low and announced that dinner was on the table. He couldn't resist a delighted grin as he spoke the words, and his white teeth gleamed in his shining black face.

"That's Favorite," Captain Young explained with a chuckle. "I brought him home from the West Indies—present to my wife. The rascal likes to put on airs."

They enjoyed a very good dinner. When it was over, and Mistress Young retired, Gid listened in rapt attention while his father and their host sipped Madeira, smoked their pipes and discussed the progress of the war.

"Our Navy's a pretty small affair compared to England's," Young admitted. "They captured four or five of our ships at Charleston, and the few frigates left aren't big enough or well enough armed to tackle a British squadron of any size. But we can harry their supply ships. What the

Board of Admiralty wants to do is get the *Trumbull*, the *Deane*, the *Confederacy* and the *Saratoga* together and break up the convoys coming from the south. The first two are on their way down from New England. The *Confederacy's* right here in port being refitted. If all goes well, we can sail the end o' June."

"You'd think," Reuben Jones suggested, "that the British would have frigates an' ships o' the line protecting those convoys."

"Right," the captain agreed. "But Admiral Arbuthnot's too busy worrying about the French fleet in the Narragansett. If he didn't keep a big squadron in those waters, he knows the French would come down and attack New York."

"The war moves slow," said Gid's father with a shake of his head. "Seems as if about all we can do is try to wear 'em down. Worst of it is, the Tory crowd's getting stronger and making more trouble down our way. Tell him about the fight you had getting the cannon up here, Gid."

The boy was embarrassed, but he gave the captain a brief account, handing most of the credit to Aaron Mathis.

Young stroked his chin and looked at him with a twinkle in his eye. "That letter from Colonel Cox," he said, "mentioned that you'd done a little fighting before. Aboard a privateer, wasn't it? Want to tell me about it?"

"Didn't amount to much," Gid replied, his face reddening. "Most o' those coasting craft surrender before you fire a shot. I did learn a bit of seamanship, though."

"Mm," said the captain. "Those winter cruises can be rough, I know. Your ship—was she square-rigged?"

"No, sir. She was just a topsail schooner—the *Rattle-snake*."

Young turned to Gid's father. "Your friend Cox, down in Batsto, seems to think quite a bit of this lad," he remarked. "In fact he's asked me if there's still room for a midshipman on the *Saratoga*. I was pretty well satisfied with the four young gentlemen we've signed, but we could certainly make room for a fifth. What would you say to the idea?"

Reuben Jones frowned. "The boy's a good iron-maker," he said. "I've been against his going to sea—wanted him to learn my own business."

"That's understandable," the captain agreed. "There's little enough profit in serving with the Navy. No prize money and uncertain pay. All it offers is a chance to fight for independence and prove to the rest of the world that these American states have the courage to become a nation."

The words were mildly spoken but they lifted Gid's heart. It had been hard for him to keep silent before. Now he glanced at his father and saw that he, too, was stirred.

The ironmaster cleared his throat. "I guess it's up to the boy to decide," he said.

Gid jumped out of his chair, his face shining. "You mean that, Dad?" he cried. "Then the answer's yes!"

CAPTAIN YOUNG'S SMILE was warm. "Good for you, my lad," he said and held out his hand. "How soon can you be back here in Philadelphia with your dunnage, ready to sail?"

"Would a week be too long?" Gid asked.

"No, I think we can give you that much time. But don't make it longer."

"Then we'd best be starting back," said Reuben Jones. "We'll be a night and another day on the road as it is."

"Stop by Satterlee's, the tailor on High Street," John Young suggested. "He can measure you for a uniform and have it finished by the time you get back."

They thanked the captain and his lady for their entertainment and set off at once. By four o'clock they were back on the New Jersey shore and had their horses saddled, ready to ride.

The trip to Batsto was completed without incident. They overtook the slow-moving wagons that had hauled the cannon on the road a few miles north of the ironworks.

Gid was delighted to see Aaron Mathis for he had been itching to tell him the news.

The burly young sailor congratulated him, but he didn't look entirely happy. For a moment Gid wondered what was troubling him. Then it came out.

"I'd sort o' hoped you'd be comin' back to the *Rattlesnake*," Aaron mumbled. "Can't blame you, though. I'd feel better about it myself if I was in the Navy. You reckon they could use a pretty fair seaman on the *Saratoga?*"

Gid let out a whoop and threw his arms around his friend. "You're mighty right they could!" he cried. "Can you be back in Philadelphia with me five days from now?"

Aaron grinned. "I'll have to go down river an' break the news to the folks," he said. "But I'll come up here in plenty o' time to make the trip."

After Gid's mother got over her first misgivings, she quickly resigned herself to the idea of Navy service for her son. There was a lot to be done before he returned to the city. She darned his hose, washed and ironed his linen and baked a cherry pie for him to eat on the way.

The boy spent his own time bidding farewell to the Mullica River country where he had grown up. He fished and swam and visited with the neighbors. On the last evening before he and Aaron were to leave he went to call at Colonel Cox's mansion. He remembered that the suggestion of a midshipman's berth for him had been made in the letter delivered to Captain Young, and he wanted to thank the colonel. Because of the heat, he left his coat at home, but the ruffles on his shirt were freshly starched and his best nankeen breeches well brushed.

Old 'Lisha opened the door at his knock and smiled a welcome.

"Sorry, suh, de Cunnel's gone out," he told Gid. "Mebbe you'll come in anyhow?"

The boy was about to refuse and go down the steps when a girl's voice came from inside.

"Who is it, 'Lisha?" she inquired. "Why don't you ask him in?"

Then she was standing beside the old serving man. Gid saw a flash of brown eyes in an attractive face, a mop of fair curls caught back with a bow, and a dimity dress with sprigs of tiny roses on it. She looked about sixteen.

"I'm Peggy Lane," she said without embarrassment. "Colonel Cox's niece. I've been at school in Burlington but it's summer holiday now, so I'm down for a visit."

She dropped him a little curtsy and he bowed somewhat awkwardly in return. "Gideon Jones," he introduced himself. "At your service, ma'am."

Before he knew just how it happened he was in the cool parlor and 'Lisha was offering them lemonade and cookies. Overcome with shyness at first, Gid soon thawed under the young lady's friendly smile. She was not only the prettiest girl he had ever seen but so gay and natural that she made him feel at ease.

Shortly he was telling her about the *Saratoga* and his new appointment.

"Oh," she said, "isn't that splendid! I know Jack Livingston and you'll be a shipmate of his. Tell me—have you ever been to sea before?"

So he described the privateer cruises and what it meant

to him to be in the regular Navy. She listened attentively and nodded approval from time to time.

"I think," she told him, "that you'll be a fine midshipman. And who knows—perhaps you'll come home a lieutenant!"

"I'd like that," he said seriously. "If I'm lucky enough not to get in the way of a cannonball or fall off a topsail yard, maybe I'll make it."

Her eyes clouded for a moment. "I forgot," she said. It *is* dangerous, isn't it? Did you say you have to go tomorrow?"

"That's right. We're taking the mail coach from Egg Harbor in the morning. So I guess I won't see you again."

She laid her hand on his impulsively. "Will you write to me?" she asked. "I'll give you the address. And I promise I'll answer every letter."

Gid drew a deep breath. "I—I'll try," he told her. "Whenever I'm in port, that is. It'll mean a lot to me if you do answer."

He got to his feet. "Reckon I'd better be going," he said. "Have to get up before daylight to make it over to Egg Harbor in time. It's—been mighty nice meeting you, Mistress Peggy."

Walking home he hardly noticed where he was going. His head was in a whirl. For a moment he half regretted the Navy duty that was taking him away just at the time he had discovered Peggy Lane. Gid had never paid much attention to girls before, and this one—the loveliest young lady he had ever seen—made his heart do flip-flops.

If only he could stay another day! But he put that

thought out of his head at once. He had promised Captain Young to be back within a week. All he could do was sigh a little and hope that the war would be over before the girl forgot him.

Aaron Mathis was at the house when he got home. It was a comfort to see his friendly grin and his sturdy, competent figure in new sailor clothes. Together they packed Gid's sea chest before their early bedtime.

It was barely dawn when Reuben Jones roused them. He had a horse harnessed to a light wagon, and at four-thirty, after a hasty breakfast, they were on the road. Two hours later they were boarding the four-horse coach in front of the tavern at Egg Harbor.

About noon on the seventeenth the two boys were landed by the ferry at the foot of High Street. Aaron undertook to find a boatman who would take them down the river to the sloop-of-war while Gid went up to Satterlee's to get his uniform. It was finished and waiting for him. He tried it on and stared at his reflection in the long mirror, squaring his shoulders, pulling in his chin and endeavoring to look as military as possible.

Much less elaborate than the dress uniform of a commissioned officer, the neat blue coat and long white pantaloons were still far handsomer than he had expected. And the brass buttons were so bright they fairly dazzled him. He kept it on, paid the tailor's bill and returned to the docks with his civilian clothes in a bundle under his arm.

Things had been happening that week, as he realized when he saw the *Saratoga*. The decks were swarming with men, all busy at the hundred tasks that go with readying a vessel for sea. Captain Young, on the quarter-deck, sighted their boat and ordered the Jacob's ladder dropped so that they could come aboard.

Gid, feeling conspicuous in his new uniform, went up the ladder first. He saluted the young lieutenant who stood waiting for them.

"Gideon Jones, midshipman, reporting for duty, sir," he said. It was a speech he had been rehearsing nervously for the past half hour, and it seemed to be the proper form. At least the lieutenant returned his salute with a straight face.

"Captain Young told me to expect you," he replied. "You'll want to stow your dunnage in the midshipmen's berth. Green, here, will show you your quarters. Glad to have you aboard." And he shook the boy's hand.

Gid gestured toward Aaron who was standing by the rail. "If you could use a good seaman, sir," he said, "I've brought one who wants to join. His name's Aaron Mathis, and he's been in ships ever since he was twelve."

The lieutenant grinned. "Use him?" he answered. "We can indeed! When you're settled I'll take you both down to sign on."

The big sailor, Patrick Green, picked up Gid's sea chest and led the way below. The midshipmen's quarters were in a small compartment just aft of the forecastle. It contained eight bunks, four on a side in double tiers, to be occupied by the master's mates and midshipmen. Gid was given the top after bunk on the port side. Aaron would sling his hammock forward with the crew.

"That was the First Lieutenant you were talkin' to,"

Green told Gid. "His name's Joshua Barney an' he's only twenty-one. But he's been five years in the Continental Navy—a mighty fine officer."

In the *Saratoga's* cabin, a few minutes later, Captain Young greeted his new midshipman and welcomed Aaron. A few questions established Aaron's fitness and he was signed as an able seaman. The swearing-in ceremonies were brief but solemn enough to make a deep impression on the two young men.

"Now," said Young, "you'll both go to work. There's plenty to be done. I want this ship ready to sail and fight by the beginning of July."

The other midshipmen, Gid discovered, were on shore leave and wouldn't return till the following week. Meanwhile, he was turned over to one of the master's mates, a rugged-looking young man named Bill Faggo, for schooling in his duties.

A midshipman in those days occupied a rather strange position. He was neither fish nor fowl. In most cases he was as green as any landlubber in the crew, yet he was supposed to be officer material as well as a gentleman. For that reason he was put through a tough course of training and harshly disciplined for every mistake. It was a hard school for any youngster who was over-proud or sensitive.

Fortunately for Gid, he had worked with his hands and was willing to take orders from men who knew more than he did. Also he was eager to learn. While he had never been to one of the aristocratic schools, he had mastered all that his country teachers could give him and he had a good mind. Best of all, he had a saving sense of humor that kept him from being ruffled by Faggo's heavy-handed criticism.

First of all he was taught the names of things. He learned every rope, every stay and halyard, every spar and sail. It wasn't easy, for in spite of her small size, the *Saratoga* was a full-rigged ship. Then came the rudiments of navigation. They were blessed with hot, clear days all that week, and Gid learned to use a sextant and shoot the sun at noon. He studied a chart of the night heavens and memorized the positions of the constellations. He sweated over mathematical calculations that seemed easy when Faggo worked them out.

In the absence of a regular gunner's mate, Charles King, a sergeant of Marines, took over Gid's training in gunnery. He had been in one of the batteries at Bunker Hill, early in the war, and knew how to train a cannon. The nine-pounders delivered from Batsto had now been mounted on wooden carriages and were ready for service.

"Some day," said King, "you may find yourself promoted to gun pointer when we're in action. That's what midshipmen are for—to move into responsible jobs when other chaps get shot. So here's how it's done."

He showed the boy how to raise the muzzle by means of a big screw under the breach. "That's for long shots. They're not much use in sea-fighting," King explained. "The real damage is done by point-blank fire, when you get in close. Then it's a matter of firing faster than the enemy."

Gid saw enough of Aaron to know that the young bayman was making a good impression. In fact he had been aboard only four days when Lieutenant Barney made him an acting bosun's mate. They stood harbor watch together the following night and Aaron told his friend about it with some pride.

"They're short o' men that know small boats," he said. "Mr. Barney asked me some questions an' found out I'd done a lot o' rowin' an' boat steerin'. So now I'm to have charge o' the longboat an' I get a raise in pay."

When he had been in the *Saratoga* a week, Gid wrote his first letter to Peggy Lane. He chose a time when there was nobody else in the midshipmen's quarters. By the light of a whale oil lantern he laid out his writing paper on the narrow deal table, sharpened a goose-quill pen, ground some ink and went to work.

It wasn't easy for him. He had written very few letters before, and none to a young lady with brown eyes and honey-blonde hair. What he wound up with was a rather stilted account of his trip to Philadelphia and his activities aboard ship. But in closing he told her he was eager to get to sea, get the war over and return to Batsto. "At which time," he added, "I trust you will permit me once more to pay my respects to your uncle and yourself." He signed it in the formal manner, "Yr. faithful obdt. svt., Gideon Jones, Midshipman, Continental Navy," sealed it with red wax and sent it off by the post next morning.

He knew he couldn't expect an early reply, for a letter would take at least three days to travel the forty-odd miles. However, she had promised to answer and he believed she meant it.

Bright and early the following Monday morning, the

officers and midshipmen who had been on leave appeared at the dockside, and two of the boats were sent to fetch them aboard. Gid was introduced to Second Lieutenant Blaney Allison, a young Philadelphian who was kin to the famous Dr. Francis Allison, late Vice Provost of the College and at one time Chaplain to the Continental Congress. The lieutenant was only a year or two older than Gid, but had served in the Navy since 1776. Taken prisoner, he had been held in the British hulks at New York for some months and had only recently been exchanged. His face was still gaunt but his prison pallor had been replaced by a healthy tan in the summer sun.

Others the boy met were the gray-haired Lieutenant of Marines, Abraham Van Dyke, John Garvin, Sailing Master, a New Hampshire man who had sailed with John Paul Jones in the *Ranger*, and Dr. William Brown, the ship's surgeon. Last of all he made the acquaintance of the four lads who were to share his experiences as a midshipman on the voyages to come.

6

Jack Livingston was a quiet youngster of eighteen, tall and slender, almost delicate in appearance. In fact, as Gid learned later, he had been an invalid through much of his boyhood. He was a rich man's son, beautifully mannered, perhaps a little spoiled. But there was strength of character in his intelligent face and no snobbishness in his attitude toward the boy from Batsto. In fact he greeted him warmly as a fellow Jerseyman.

Oldest of the midshipmen was Barent Sebring, who joined the *Saratoga* at twenty-three. He was a cousin of Mistress Young, and his appointment had come through the captain. He took himself seriously, but was wholly unacquainted with the sea.

Nat Penfield, from Connecticut, had sailed in privateers and knew more seamanship than any of the other four. He talked with a Yankee twang that caused some amusement among his mates, but he was a big, good-natured fellow of twenty-one, able to take care of himself.

Gid took an immediate liking to the last of the new

midshipmen. Sam Clarkson, youngest of them all, was still under eighteen. He was the son of a noted Philadelphia physician. His sea service was limited to a brief voyage to Martinique in the frigate *Confederacy*, but he was so active and lively that he had picked up a fair smattering of nautical experience. There was an impish quality in the boy's character that constantly got him into trouble, yet he was so likable that he was usually let off with nothing more than a light reprimand. Gid sensed all this within five minutes. He knew life would never be monotonous with Sam Clarkson around.

All through the month of July the *Saratoga* remained in port, waiting for her sailing orders. Captain Young chafed at the delay. He knew his ship was ready, and he was anxious to give his green crew some seasoning at sea before they were called upon to fight.

They were waiting, Gid heard through the ship's grapevine, for work to be completed in refitting the *Confederacy*, which now lay at a yard up the river. Also two frigates were daily expected from New England—the *Deane* and the *Trumbull*. It was the idea of the Board of Admiralty that all three of these vessels, in company with the new *Saratoga*, should operate as a fleet to harry British shipping along the coast. Or, if it seemed more profitable, they could join forces with Admiral de Ternay's French squadron which, at the moment, was blockaded in Narragansett Bay.

The trouble was the usual one—money. There weren't enough funds to finish the work on the *Confederacy*, and the other two ships were slow in arriving.

So the captain had to content himself with drilling the crew each day while the sloop-of-war lay at anchor. It was hard, heavy work, and the sultry heat of early August made it still more tiresome. There was grumbling among some of the landsmen, but firm discipline kept them at their tasks. And at last, on the 11th of August, some relief from the routine was promised.

On that day a messenger from the Board of Admiralty came aboard and delivered a sealed packet to Captain Young. The rumor spread quickly that he must have received sailing orders, and the look on his face, when he appeared on deck, confirmed the feeling. He was no longer frowning and depressed. His eyes sparkled and he grinned as he spoke to Lieutenant Barney.

Almost immediately the word was passed that the midshipmen would be given twenty-four hours shore leave, with strict orders to be back aboard by six o'clock the following evening. Young Sam Clarkson was jubilant. "That means we're sailing, right enough," he told his mates. "But it gives us tonight for a party at my house. Shine your shoes, wash your faces and put on your best bibs and tuckers. I'll send word to have the carriage pick us up at three o'clock."

Gid took a swim over the side to cool off, then had a seaman douse him with a bucket of fresh water. He toweled his hair, combed it out, and tied it behind with a bit of narrow black ribbon. Clean linen and his one pair of silk hose were put on. Then came the smart new breeches and the brass-buttoned uniform coat. For his first venture into

Philadelphia society he wanted to look as well as the others and he succeeded.

Promptly at three the carriage appeared. It was a green barouche, drawn by a pair of handsome black horses and driven by a plump Negro coachman. Bubbling with high spirits, the five youngsters piled in. They were borne northward to Walnut Street, then turned west up the hill. Ten minutes later the carriage rolled up in front of a spacious brick house with a garden and stables that filled most of the block.

An elderly butler opened the door and showed the young gentlemen to their rooms. Sam Clarkson had invited Gid to share his own quarters.

"There'll be a houseful tonight," he explained. "Soon as Mother heard we were coming she decided we'd need a few o' the fair sex about to liven things up. If I don't mistake I can hear 'em twittering now."

Below, in the drawing room, Mistress Clarkson was waiting to receive the boys. She was a vivacious little lady with snapping black eyes and a quick, friendly smile. Gid felt at ease with her, for she was very much like her son.

The other three midshipmen came down in a few moments, and shortly after that a bevy of pretty girls appeared. The rest of the young men were already acquainted with them but Gid had to be introduced. Jack's sisters, Sue and Kitty Livingston, were among them. And the names of the others were familiar to him, for these were daughters of leading families. They were dressed in the latest mode, and their conversation was full of such fashionable expressions as "La, sir!" and arch references to the balls and assemblies of the past winter.

There were four of these self-assured young ladies. They soon paired off with the other midshipmen, and Gid, listening to their laughing chatter, felt a bit out of his depth. Sam glanced his way, saw his sober face and grinned sympathetically.

Without delay he brought a dark, attractive girl over to his friend. "Gid," he said, "I've an errand to do for Mother. Won't you take Nancy out and show her the rose garden?"

The Batsto boy bowed and offered the girl his arm. A moment later they were outside the French doors, strolling on a velvety lawn. He struggled to find a polite and appropriate remark, but Nancy Breckinridge came to his rescue.

"I wonder," she said, studying his face with interest, "if you're not the very same young man."

Gid looked at her, confused. The remark seemed to make no sense.

"I mean," she continued, "it was in a letter from a schoolmate of mine—you know—Mistress Drake's Female Seminary, in Burlington. She's been off on a visit, somewhere down in the Jersey wilds, but she said she'd met a handsome sailor. You *are* in the *Saratoga*, aren't you?"

Gid flushed under his tan. "Is—is your friend's name Peggy Lane?" he asked.

Nancy laughed. "Then you *are* the one. How romantic! I can't wait to write Peg and tell her I've seen you."

The boy was saved from further embarrassment by the sudden arrival of the rest of the party.

"We're going to have tea out here in the summer house," Sam announced. "It's cooler than indoors. Heavens, Gid, what's this baggage been telling you? You're red as a beet!"

Nancy laughed merrily. "We've got a secret, haven't we, Mr. Jones?" she said. And there the matter dropped.

They had a large and appetizing meal, topped off with a special Philadelphia dessert that was new to Gid. It was called ice cream. Given the chance, he thought he could have kept on eating the delicious stuff all night.

Later there was dancing that lasted till two in the morning, and the boys slept till nearly noon. There was less hilarity when the party assembled for a late breakfast. All the midshipmen must have felt, as Gid did, that this marked the end of a period in their lives. Tomorrow they would be under sail, headed toward unknown toils and dangers. Some of them, perhaps, might not come back.

The girls, too, seemed to sense it, for they were quieter and more thoughtful.

When the time came to leave, Mistress Clarkson kissed her son and each of his friends in turn and wished them Godspeed with tenderness but without tears. Some of the girls were dabbing their eyes with handkerchiefs. Nancy Breckinridge pressed Gid's hand at parting.

"I'll tell her," she whispered. "And I'm sure she'll write to you."

* * *

By six o'clock that evening, when the ship's bell struck for the beginning of the second dog watch, the officers and men of the crew were mustered aft. Lieutenant Barney called the roll and all answered but one—a seaman who went by the odd name of Anthony Castoff.

"I seen him in the Tarpot Tavern," one of the sailors volunteered. "Well potted he was, too."

Sergeant King and two marines were sent to search the waterfront grog shops for the missing man, and all the rest lined up at attention. Then the captain mounted the quarter-deck.

"We're going to see whether you're fit to be called a crew," he announced cheerfully. "We'll be dropping down river on the morning's tide. Our orders are secret, but I think I may promise you a bit of action. This is your last full night's sleep, so make the most of it. From now on you'll be standing regular watches."

They cheered as he turned back to the companionway. Barney detailed a dozen men to harbor watch duty and the rest of them went below. The air was a little cooler that night and there was a gentle stir of breeze through the 'tween-decks. A good night for sleeping, Gid thought. But it was a long time before he slept. The anticipation of putting to sea was too strong in his mind.

When he woke it was early daylight and the bosun's pipe was shrilling on deck. "Roll out, ye lubbers," the man bawled in a bull voice. "Rise an' shine!"

Sam Clarkson had brought a basket of peaches from home, and each of the midshipmen ate one to piece out a skimpy breakfast of hardtack and tea. The men were hard at work holystoning the deck, coiling down ropes and putting the vessel in order. A few last provisions were hurried aboard. The tide would start to ebb at ten o'clock.

It was nearing that hour when the tired-looking marine detail returned. They had been out all night hunting for the missing Castoff. Now they had him, and they hustled him aboard with some roughness. One of the few Negroes in the crew, his thin, haggard face was so miserable that Gid felt sorry for him. But he was put to work at once and given a taste of the rope's end to start him moving.

John Garvin, the Master, had been watching the slack water off the bow. Occasionally he tossed a bit of stick over the side. At last the chip he threw moved southward with the turn of the tide, and he ordered half a dozen hands to the capstan. As the cable began to come in, the topmen went aloft and all preparations were made to get sail on her.

At that moment a big open carriage came rumbling over the cobbles to the dockside. The *Saratoga* lay a hundred yards offshore, but even at that distance Gid recognized the pretty faces under the wide-brimmed bonnets. It was Mistress Clarkson with the same four young ladies who had been at the party.

Not only the midshipmen but the whole crew waved and cheered. Then the topsails caught the breeze, the ship came up smartly and the dripping anchor was hoisted clear of the water.

"Helm hard over!" Faggo sang out to the man at the wheel. The deck heeled a little and the ship moved gracefully out into the river, her bow swinging seaward.

There was a light wind from the west, and as the Delaware made a bend to the westward a little way below the city, the ship had to run close-hauled, skirting the Jersey shore. Within an hour she came in sight of the chevaux-de-frise, a barrier of spiked stakes that had been set in the channel to prevent enemy ships from reaching Philadelphia. Here the captain himself stood by while the pilot took his vessel through the twisting passage. Early in the afternoon they hove to off the port of Chester.

There were several ships moored there and among them Gid saw a tall-masted craft with rakish lines, apparently getting ready for sea. Jack Livingston was studying her through his spyglass.

"She's the packet *Mercury*," he announced after a moment. "Fastest ship in America, they say. She's signaling us, too. Can you read those flags?"

Gid tried to spell out the message but he had only one or two lessons in the code and was unable to get more than a few words. "I think they're sending a boat," he replied. "Yes—look there—someone's coming over to us."

As the other ship's gig swept over the water, Barney ordered the side boys piped to their places. All were standing at attention when their visitor came up the ladder. He was a distinguished-looking gray-haired man, elegantly dressed. Gid heard the lieutenant greet him as "Mr. Laurens" before escorting him aft.

"I've met him," young Livingston whispered excitedly. "He's Henry Laurens, of South Carolina—a mighty important man in the Congress. He's going to Europe on some secret mission, and unless I'm much mistaken we may be sent along to convoy his ship!"

For the better part of an hour, Mr. Laurens was closeted with the captain. When he left, John Young came with him to the ship's side and they shook hands cordially.

"Tomorrow, then," the boys heard their skipper remark. "We'll plan to make sail early and use the tide. I know you'd like to clear the Capes while this weather holds."

There was a good deal of excitement in the midshipmen's berth that evening. A voyage to France was something none of them had dreamed of till now. Yet the more they talked about it the more plausible Jack's guess seemed.

Gid's watch had the deck from eight to twelve that night. He watched the sun go down behind the Brandywine hills and wondered what it would be like to walk the streets of a foreign city where nobody spoke any English.

He mentioned the subject to Aaron, who came up to stand beside him by the rail. But the young bosun's mate had a different idea about their destination. He had got it from Faggo, who had his information from Garvin.

"This here's a fightin' ship," said Aaron. "Once we're offshore the *Mercury* won't need us, 'cause nothin' under the British flag is fast enough to overhaul her. The way I hear it, we're s'posed to jine up with the *Trumbull* an' *Deane* an' put in some licks against the king's supply lines. Honest, now—wouldn't you rather do that than go wanderin' 'round amongst them French monsoors?"

And Gid quickly admitted that he would.

As soon as the tide favored, next morning, the two ships stood down the river in company. They were just off Bombay Hook when the headsails of a pair of large vessels were sighted, heading up Delaware Bay from the south.

Captain Young took no chances. He hove to in mid-channel and told his lieutenants to clear for action. The *Mercury* meanwhile retreated toward Port Penn. But five minutes later the bustle of preparation aboard the sloop-of-war was interrupted. Both the approaching ships had hoisted the Stars and Stripes, and it was soon apparent that they were the long-awaited frigates from New England.

The captain ordered the gig lowered and hurried over to the *Mercury* for a conference with Laurens, while signals were made to the *Deane* and the *Trumbull* to stand by. As soon as Young returned he sent a boat with a letter from the Board of Admiralty to the *Trumbull's* captain, James Nicholson.

The boat was halfway back to the sloop-of-war when signal flags broke out aboard the frigate. The midshipmen read them stumblingly but with interest.

"Both ships short of water," the flags announced. "Will proceed Philadelphia for supplies. Return without delay."

Gid glanced at the quarter-deck and saw a scowl on Captain Young's face. Apparently the answer was disappointing to him.

They all found out why in the days that followed. It should have been possible for the two frigates to reach port, fill their casks and come back down the bay in forty-eight hours. But the second day passed and the third, and no sails were sighted.

Eager to get to sea, the skipper of the *Saratoga* paced up and down with jaw set. He was gruff with his officers and they in turn were harsh in handling the crew. The men were kept on the jump all day, painting, scrubbing decks and polishing brass.

Finally, on the fourth morning, Young went over to the packet for another consultation with Henry Laurens. Gid watched the boat coming back across the strip of blue water and knew that some decision had been reached. The men at the oars were pulling hard and bending their backs to it. In the stern-sheets the captain's face was smiling for the first time in days.

"Mr. Barney," he told the first lieutenant as he came over the side, "you may get sail on her at once."

There was an immediate shrilling of pipes and shouting of orders as the topmen scurried aloft. Over on the *Mercury* white canvas was already fluttering out of the gaskets.

The wind stood fair from the northwest, and within a few minutes the two ships were sweeping down the bay under full sail.

The port watch, to which Gid was assigned, went below for supper at six o'clock. But the boy was too excited to stay in the 'tween-decks. Well before the end of the second dog watch he was on deck to see them clear the Capes. In the sunset haze it was impossible to make out Cape May, to the eastward. However, a bluff headland stood out of the sea to starboard, and that, he knew, must be Cape Henlopen.

At eight bells, when the rest of the watch appeared, Lieutenant Barney mustered them amidships.

"I want double lookouts tonight," he told them sternly. "Mr. Jones, you'll take the foremast cross-trees. And keep alive every minute. If there are British cruisers about, we're likely to find 'em within a few leagues o' the Capes. It'll be a good, clear night—no fog. Now get aloft, an' sing out fast if you sight a sail."

Thrilled with his orders, Gid hurried up the ratlines and took his place on the lofty perch above the fore-yard. Half a mile ahead, over the port bow, the *Mercury* dipped gracefully over the swells. The sun was gone, but a ruddy afterglow tinted the packet's towering canvas with pink and gold against a backdrop of purple sea. Reluctantly the boy drew his eyes away from her and searched the horizon north and south with grim intensity. He had to keep telling himself it was on just such pretty nights as this that sea fights took place. And if there had been a leak—if the enemy knew a leading patriot on a secret mission was in their convoy—there would surely be a king's frigate standing off the coast.

After an hour in which no hostile sails were sighted, Gid noticed one thing that troubled him. The *Mercury* was pulling steadily away from them. He hailed the deck, and Aaron's voice answered.

"The packet's a good mile ahead now," Gid reported. "Shouldn't we be staying closer?"

The young bosun's mate passed the word to the officer of the deck and a moment later the order was given to set royals and studding sails. The *Saratoga* responded with more apparent speed but she didn't seem to gain. When Gid was relieved, midway through the watch, he had to point twice in the darkness before Sam Clarkson could find the small, distant outline of the packet's sails.

Lieutenant Barney was aft by the binnacle. He seemed dissatisfied with the way the ship was handling. Gid heard him criticize the quartermaster sharply. Then he took the wheel himself. After a few minutes he sent Gid to bring John Garvin, the Sailing Master.

The two officers consulted in low tones and tried several changes of sail. The ship did less yawing when her mizzen royal was taken off, but she still refused to log as much speed as she should with a good wind and a following sea.

It was close to eight bells and the watch was about to be changed when Clarkson's hail came from the crosstrees.

"Sail-ho on the starboard bow!" he cried. "It's the *Mercury*. She's come up into the wind—waiting for us, I guess."

Barney hurried forward and confirmed the midship-

man's report. The packet stayed there until the *Saratoga* drew abeam, then fell off before the wind again. She was within hailing distance.

"What's the matter there?" her skipper roared through his speaking trumpet. "Can't you make more speed—or do we have to take in sail?"

Barney's reply was sheepish. "We're doing the best we can, Captain Pickles," he said. "She just isn't fast enough before the wind."

They could hear the packet's commander snort in answer. "I thought your ship was supposed to be a smart sailer! Or is it the way you handle her? We're in danger here, man—let's be going!"

The lieutenant held his temper in check and turned from the rail without making any reply. Every man in the watch had heard the exchange and was burning with indignation. Yet Gid had to admit, as he went below, that the *Saratoga* wasn't living up to the promise of her fast and beautiful lines.

Below in his bunk, Gid was slow going to sleep. He could feel the vessel straining, putting forth all she had, and he prayed she would redeem herself. For to him this new ship was more than just a sloop-of-war. She was his first love—a symbol of his patriotic fervor.

When he was roused out, at four in the morning, Gid still had the matter on his mind. On deck he found a glum group in the starboard watch. Jack Livingston shook his head as he passed him on the way below.

"Hope she'll do better for you than she has for us," the

governor's son whispered. "Captain Young's fair tearing his hair out, trying to get more knots out of her."

Sure enough, Gid saw the square, determined figure of the captain by the wheel. He was frowning as he glanced first aloft at the draw of the sails, then ahead toward the fast-moving *Mercury*. Every few minutes he would call to the man with the log-line.

"What d' ye make, Thompson?"

"Eight knots, sir. Maybe a bit better."

Gid thought he could hear the skipper grit his teeth. "Eight knots!" he growled. "And with this breeze she should be making ten!"

The first gray of dawn was in the sky before the boy's watch ended. Forward all eyes were focused on the topsails of the packet, now hardly more than a white speck on the horizon.

"She must be at least four miles in the lead," Sam Clarkson muttered. "We might as well be sailing a washtub!"

"Don't say that," Gid flared. "You wait. They'll find out what the trouble is before the day's out, I'll warrant."

When they returned to the deck at eight o'clock, a council of the top officers was in progress, aft. Gid wasn't near enough to overhear any of the arguments put forth, but it was obvious that Captain Young held a strong opinion and was trying to convince Garvin and the two lieutenants. Meanwhile the *Mercury* was hove to again, waiting for them to come up.

When they were within hailing distance, Young himself used the speaking trumpet.

"Captain Pickles," he shouted, "we're unable to hold pace with you."

"Yes," the other skipper replied sarcastically. "So I've noticed."

"I think I've discovered the trouble," Young continued. "We need more ballast. Would you be good enough to ask Mr. Laurens to come on deck?"

The statesman appeared, a moment later, and Captain Young addressed him.

"Sir," he said, "you'll make better time and be safer if you leave us here. We're a hundred miles offshore. I doubt if you'll see any British sail from this point on."

Laurens took a minute or two before replying. Then his voice was cold and aloof.

"Your orders, sir," he said, "are to accompany me in convoy beyond the zone of danger. I consider that this zone has not yet been passed. Kindly make the best speed you can and let us continue at once."

The man's icy tone left little room for argument. "Very well, sir," John Young replied, and both ships fell off before the wind.

For two more days they continued eastward. Each evening the *Mercury* was leagues ahead and had to heave to so that the sloop-of-war wouldn't lose her in the darkness. Through the night they stayed close together, the packet under shortened sail. It was a humiliating business for every man aboard the *Saratoga*. On occasions when they were near enough they had to take the gibes of the packet's crew without answering. To relieve their feelings they worked furiously at whatever tasks were given them.

For several hours each day they were occupied with gun practice. Gid had been put in charge of one of the nine-pounder cannon in the port battery, the second gun from the stern. He had a crew of three men to whip into shape. Only one of them was an experienced cannoneer. He was a big, slow-moving seaman named Tom Pilkinton, who had been in other naval vessels. Jack Caligan was Irish, a lean, wiry little man with a shiftless streak in him. The third member of the group was the queer character who had overstayed his shore leave in Philadelphia—the Negro called Anthony Castoff.

Gid never felt quite at ease with him. His skin looked gray and he was hollow-chested, with sunken cheeks and bony arms. His eyes always had a faraway look, and they stared out of deep caverns beneath his stringy, lank black hair. Most of the crew thought he was crazy or half-witted. Such was the material the young midshipman had to work with.

He knew he could count on Pilkinton, but the man had no initiative. He was used to doing only what he was ordered. Caligan was a shirker who had to be watched constantly. And Castoff, though he had surprising strength in his thin arms, moved about like a man in a dream.

A dozen times during each practice session the guns were pulled in by the tackle, swabbed out, loaded with powder bags and round shot, then run out again and pointed. Every part of the drill was real except for actual firing.

While these exercises went on, Second Lieutenant Allison stood amidships with watch in hand. His yell started all the gun captains together and the better crews worked like lightning to be first. For a dozen rounds Gid's gun was among the last run out. He did his utmost to get more speed out of his men but the harder they tried the more they seemed to get in one another's way.

Marine Sergeant King saw the boy's exasperation and came over to him when there was a break in the routine. Gid explained his difficulties and the sergeant nodded.

"They're a mismatched lot," he said, "but maybe ye can make a team of 'em yet. Take big Tom, now. He's strong —a good man on the tackle. Don't let him wait for an order. Just make him understand that when ye slap him on the back he's to pull. That Caligan, now, he hates work but he's quick as a monkey when he wants to be. Promise him a chaw o' tobacco an' he'll handle powder an' shot for ye in a hurry. That leaves the swabbin' to Castoff, an' I guess that's about all he's good for. Ye'll train the gun yerself, o' course."

Gid thought over the advice and resolved to give it a try. Chewing tobacco was, he knew, a favorite habit of most seamen. He had no wish to try it himself, but for a shilling he purchased a long black twist of the stuff from the ship's stores. Before they started another gun drill he gathered his men around the breech of the cannon, telling each what he was to do.

"Our time's been mighty slow," he said. "Around twenty-five or thirty seconds. Some o' the best crews are making it in twenty. Now, Jack"—he turned to Caligan— "I'm giving you the toughest job of all—loading. That's because one o' the other midshipmen laughed at our time and said an Irishman couldn't work fast. I don't believe it. The first time we break twenty seconds I'll give you all you can bite off this plug. Is it a bargain?"

Caligan's response was a twisted grin but there was a gleam in his eye. Whether it was resentment at the slur on the Irish or the bribe Gid had offered, the little seaman underwent a surprising change when the word was given to start. He sprang to his work like a fury, ready to ram home the powder bag the instant the swab was pulled from the muzzle. The others, too, responded with more speed. And instead of trailing the rest of the battery they were ready almost at the same moment as the winning gun.

"Nineteen seconds for Number Five!" Lieutenant Allison announced. "And Number Two, you were right behind 'em. Smart work, there, Mr. Jones! All right—draw your charges."

Solemnly Gid drew the big twist of tobacco from his pocket and held it out to Caligan. The little Irishman saluted, then bit off such a monstrous chew that Gid stared in disbelief. But remembering his promise he couldn't complain. The new speed of his gun crew was worth it.

THE *Saratoga* remained in company with the packet for
more than a week. Finally, on the morning of the 23rd of
August, Henry Laurens signaled once more for Captain
Young to come aboard. The gig lay at the *Mercury's*
boarding ladder for nearly two hours, while the two were
closeted in the cabin. When the captain came back he answered his mate's greeting with a smile.

"At last," he said, "the convoy's done. We're free to
make a cruise on our own. Get sail on her and give the
helmsman a course for the Carolinas."

The order was carried out briskly. Before noon the topgallantsails of the packet had vanished over the horizon
and the sloop-of-war was bowling south by west with a
good wind abeam.

Young and Garvin continued to experiment with the
ship's rig and ballast as they voyaged toward home waters.
They tried shifting the stores in the hold and reefing or
trimming sails. But the fact was that she still handled
badly whenever she carried enough canvas for speed.

Some of the newer hands were afraid they had landed in an unseaworthy ship but the more experienced seamen laughed at them.

"There's nothin' wrong with her," said Pat Green, "that a few tons o' rock or broken cannon won't cure. The skipper knows it, but he hates to go back to port without a prize or two."

The drills in gunnery and seamanship continued as long as the weather held fair. The officers were in no hurry to tackle the coastwise shipping and possible British cruisers until they had whipped a crew into shape. So for two weeks they moved slowly south and west, keeping a weather eye out for the hurricanes that might be expected soon.

For days the water had been deep blue and the air balmy, as they crossed the Gulf Stream. Whenever the men weren't busy they fished with handlines over the rail, and once they ran through a school of small tuna that snapped hungrily at any bait. That night the black cook, who went by the high-sounding name of Prince Gilbert, made chowder for supper and all hands ate till they were fairly bursting.

Gid had succeeded in keeping his gun crew on its toes. At least Caligan, who had the most important job, was working fast and well. That much had been accomplished by a combination of good-natured gibes and further offers of tobacco. Pilkinton, too, was making better speed on the tackle now that he knew what he was expected to do. The only one who worried Gid was Castoff. The man did what was demanded of him but there was no snap in his movements, no eagerness in his face. He went through the required motions as if he were walking in his sleep. Sometimes a cough racked his thin body so that he could barely hold the handle of the swab.

One night on watch, Gid went forward to check the bow lookout and almost stumbled over a figure huddled by the capstan. There was a chill in the air that night. They were out of the Gulf Stream and nearing the Carolina coast. The man crouching there was wrapped in a blanket and Gid recognized the gaunt face that looked miserably up at him.

"What are you doing on deck, Castoff?" he asked sharply. "You're in the starboard watch, aren't you?"

"Aye, sir," the sailor answered in a hoarse whisper. "But 'twas stuffy in the fo'c's'le. I wanted air. It's cold, though—awful cold!"

Gid was about to tell him to go below but a feeling of pity made him hesitate.

"What's wrong?" he asked, more gently. "You aren't sick, are you?"

Anthony Castoff was staring out to sea. He nodded slowly. "I've been sick for a long while," he said. "Can't hardly get my breath sometimes."

"You shouldn't have sailed on this voyage. What made you enlist?"

The hollow sound that came in answer might have been a cough or a laugh.

"Didn't have no other place to go," said Castoff. "An' no work to keep me."

"Don't you have a trade? How did you get along before?"

There was a long wait before the low-voiced reply came.
"I was a painter."

"But," said Gid, "there's plenty of work ashore—painting houses an' signs an' ships."

Castoff's thin shoulders shook in a spasm of shivering.
"Not that kind o' painting," he murmured. "Portraits—
miniatures, mostly. And some landscapes and sunsets. Not
the kind o' thing you get regular pay for. A bit o' food,
maybe, or an old coat or a pair o' shoes. That's what I got
for my pictures—'cause I'm colored, I reckon."

Gid swallowed, finding no words to say. At last he
turned away. "I—I'd like to see some of 'em some time,"
he threw back over his shoulder.

When the watch ended and he returned to his berth in
the 'tween-decks, he still had the sick sailor on his mind.
He slept badly that night. And in the morning he went
aft and asked permission to speak to Lieutenant Barney.

"It's about a man in my gun crew, sir," Gid said.
"There's something wrong with him. He's sick—lung
fever, I'd guess. Maybe you'd say something about it to
the surgeon, sir. His name's Anthony Castoff."

The lieutenant looked thoughtful. "I've noticed him,
too," he answered. "I'll ask Dr. Brown to take a look at
him."

There was no drilling at the guns that morning. The
sea ran choppy and gray and occasional rain squalls came
out of the northeast. The reefers and topmen were kept
busy aloft. More than that, they could expect to sight

coastwise ships at any time now, and the captain ordered double lookouts posted.

Late in the afternoon, Sam Clarkson, in the fore top, spotted a sail to the northwest. The helm was put over and the *Saratoga* set out in pursuit of the other ship. The Yankee colors were lowered and the decks cleared. Captain Young wanted to know more about the stranger before he committed himself.

Gid felt a tingling all through him as he stood in the bows with the eager crew and watched the chase through scudding rain. The sky cleared after a while but daylight was nearly gone before the ship was close enough to be identified. She was a good-sized brig and there was no mistaking the British flag flying at her main truck.

At once the men of the *Saratoga* were called to battle stations. The cannon were shotted and run out, tubs of sea water were filled, ready to fight fire, and the gun captains looked to their priming and lighted their slow-matches. Gid's mouth felt dry. He was in the port battery, and he knew they would try to keep the weather gauge to windward of the brig. That meant the port side would be firing first if it came to a fight.

From the quarter-deck Young hailed the other vessel as they drew abreast.

"What brig is that?" he called.

"His Majesty's brig *Keppel*, John Steel commanding. Charlestown for New York. Who are you?"

Every man on deck held his breath as the Yankee captain replied.

"This is the Continental sloop-of-war *Saratoga*," he

said. The dim light of the battle lanterns shone on striped bunting as the flag was run up to the peak.

"Heave to," Young shouted, "or I open fire!"

Footing faster than the other ship, the *Saratoga* was already slightly ahead and little more than a cable's length to windward. Now, in a sudden maneuver, the British skipper swung the brig sharply to starboard to cut astern of the sloop-of-war. But Young was equally quick. He gave an instant order to the helm to fall off to port, and seconds later he commanded the port battery to fire.

Gid drew a deep breath, sighted along his cannon and held the match ready. As the guns began to bear they roared out a ragged salvo. The broadside was answered immediately by the brig's cannon, but neither vessel appeared much damaged. A tossing sea and inexperienced gunners made clean hits scarce. While the *Saratoga* came about the port gun crews hauled, swabbed and reloaded with all the speed their drills had taught them. From across the deck the starboard battery thundered. Then the ship heeled on the opposite tack and once more it was time for Gid to fire. It was hard to find the target in the sights. The gale was gaining in force and the deck heaved and fell away disconcertingly. The boy tried to time his fire, but as he touched the match to the priming hole he knew he had waited too long. The round shot went screaming high into the brig's rigging.

So it went for several exchanges. There were a few holes in the *Saratoga's* sails and one of the backstays had parted. The *Keppel* seemed to be in no worse shape. Impatient

with the results of his broadsides, Captain Young ordered grappling irons made ready and had Lieutenant Van Dyke line his marines up along the rail. He meant to carry the brig by boarding.

The smoky light of the lanterns must have been enough to show the enemy captain what was in progress. Immediately the brig sheered off, well out of reach of the grappling hooks. Again and again Young tried to close with his quarry, but the brig's crew handled her too well.

Fuming, the Yankee captain went back to gunfire. He had all the cannon loaded with chain-shot in an effort to cripple the other ship by carrying away a mast. But with the weather growing steadily worse there was no improvement in the *Saratoga's* gunnery. One shot struck the brig's deck and they saw men fall. That was the only sign of serious damage the lookouts could report.

The battle went on for three hours. At last, after still another effort to take the brig by boarding, Captain Young decided to break off the engagement. Most of their powder and shot was gone and it looked as if victory was out of reach. They trimmed their sails and veered off before the wind into the darkness.

Nobody aboard the *Saratoga* was happy after her first fight with the enemy. The mates growled about the gunnery and the sailing master was disgusted over the way the ship had been out-maneuvered. The boys in the midshipmen's berth wore long faces. Each of them blamed himself for some part of the fiasco. In Gid's mind there was no doubt about it, for he felt sure that if he had another chance he could put a shot into the hull of the brig. Fortunately he was tired enough to fall asleep without worrying.

Back on deck before dawn, he found the wind had gone down, though the sea was still running heavily. The ship's carpenter and the bosun's mates were already busy repairing minor damage to the spars and rigging. Then, as soon as the sun rose, the captain ordered more sail put on. The course was laid straight for the Delaware Capes and a favoring wind sent them northwestward at a steady pace.

By the end of the second day the crew had recovered some of their good spirits. They were heading home, and even though they had little to boast about, they could look forward to a day or two of shore leave.

Gid had the first watch, the night of September 12. He was called aft and assigned to the wheel, along with the old seaman, Patrick Green.

"Won't be long now," Pat told him. "By our last reckonin' we're only ten or twelve leagues sou'east o' Cape Henlopen. Here—it's easy steerin' tonight—you take her a spell."

Gid had done only a few tricks at the wheel, and took hold of the spokes with some misgiving. However, he found Green had been right. The southwest breeze was right abeam and the vessel had less tendency to yaw than when she was running before the wind. There was still light enough for him to watch the draw of the sails, and under the binnacle lamp he could see that his compass bearing varied hardly a point.

When two bells announced the end of the first hour, Green took over the helm once more. Gid was standing beside him, staring ahead into the darkness that hid the coast. The hail of the forward lookout came back to them faintly above the creak of cordage.

"Deck, ho! Sail!"

"Where away?" called Barney.

"Dead ahead, sir—about a mile. Can't make her out but I'd say she's runnin' north before the wind."

Sam Clarkson came aft on the run with orders to call the captain. And a moment later Young was on the quarter-deck.

He ordered the sheets slacked and the course shifted to intercept the other vessel. Meanwhile Barney himself had gone up the fore shrouds with a glass for a better view of the stranger. Shortly he came back to report.

"Looks like a snow," Gid heard him say. "Two-masted and square-rigged, with what I'd judge was a trysail aft. We're gaining on her fast."

"Good," said Young. "Call all hands to stations. I doubt if she'll fight, but we must be ready."

Soon they were near enough so that all could make out the shape of the other vessel. Gid stood by his gun, hoping for a chance to improve his marksmanship. He was disappointed when he saw the snow at close quarters. She was small, slow-moving and apparently unarmed.

The captain hailed her. "What ship is that?"

"British snow *Sarah*, bound from Nevis to New York. Are you on the king's side?"

"This is the Continental sloop-of-war *Saratoga*," Young snapped back. "Heave to and surrender!"

There was no show of resistance. Meekly and promptly

the *Sarah* swung up into the wind, her grimy sails slatting. Young ordered the longboat launched and sent Second Lieutenant Blaney Allison over with a prize crew. Captain McKinley, who was in command of the snow, and all the dozen men aboard her were brought back to the *Saratoga* as prisoners.

By midnight, when Gid's watch went below, the whole affair was over and the two ships were sailing westward in company. They were well inside the Delaware Capes when daylight came. Allison crowded on all the sail the snow would carry and managed to keep within hailing distance of the *Saratoga*. He had had a chance to read the *Sarah's* manifest and check on what was in her hold. What he found was surprising. Without a shot being fired, they had taken a cargo of two hundred and thirty-four puncheons of the best West India rum—a prize that was worth a small fortune!

ONE MONTH to the day from the time she had sailed from Philadelphia, the *Saratoga* came back to her home port. She had anchored off Chester in the early morning to wait for a helping tide and a post rider was sent off to report her return. With that advance notice there was a fair crowd collected at the dock in Southwark to greet the ship as she came in.

A little apart from the group of sailors' wives and long-shoremen Gid saw a distinguished figure in a broadcloth coat, lace ruffles and powdered wig pacing the wharf impatiently.

"That's Francis Lewis," Jack Livingston told him. "Chairman of the Board of Admiralty and a great friend of Captain Young. There'll be much they'll want to talk over, I'll wager."

No sooner was the anchor dropped and the sails furled than the captain ordered his gig lowered. Aaron Mathis, who had been ashore at Chester earlier in the day, grinned at Gid as they watched Lewis hurry to meet their skipper.

"Good thing we happened across that snow," the bayman chuckled. "From what I heard down river the *Confederacy's* still hung up for want o' money to refit her.
Now maybe the Board of Admiralty can get hold o' some
cash. That prize rum ought to bring plenty."

All hands were kept aboard that night, but the next day
about half of the crew were given shore leave. Gid wasn't
one of the lucky ones. However, as he had no place in particular to go, it made little difference to him. There was
ample work to keep him busy. Shortly after noon a pro-
cession of lighters began moving from shore to the ship.
Some brought provisions and took back water casks to be
filled. Others carried new supplies of powder and shot.

Among the things hoisted aboard was a small sack of
mail, and when it had been sorted Gid found two letters
addressed to him. That night when he was alone in the
midshipmen's berth he opened and read them. One was
from his mother, full of small news and love and prayers
for his safety. The other, written in a firm, round girlish
hand, had also come by coach from Batsto.

Gid broke the seal with shaking fingers. Even now,
though the letter was dated three weeks earlier, he thought
it held a faint, sweet fragrance. He hardly needed to look
at the signature to know it was from Peggy Lane.

It was a formal little note, thanking him for his letter
and wishing him well. There were one or two references
to dances and parties at the colonel's mansion which gave
the boy a twinge of jealousy. But the main thing was that
she had written, as she promised. He took pen and paper
at once and replied with a long letter, describing his first

cruise as a midshipman. He was honest about the fight with the *Keppel,* admitting that the sloop-of-war's gunnery had left something to be desired. But he vowed his ship would give a better account of herself the next time they met the enemy.

The next day it was Gid's turn to go ashore. He posted his letter, wandered about the town and found his way to the State House where the Congress was in session. Of course he didn't venture inside, but stared in awe at the rows of fine carriages and riding horses hitched at posts along the street. After a simple meal in a tavern at noon he walked westward to the Clarkson house.

The butler remembered him and showed him in. He sat for ten minutes in the big library, marveling at the rows on rows of books that filled the shelves. Then there was a rustle of silk at the door and Mistress Clarkson entered. She smiled as she saw him.

"Why, it's Mr. Gideon Jones!" she said. "I suppose you've come to find Sam. Too bad—he left for the ship not an hour ago."

Gid bowed over her hand. "No, Ma'am," he told her. "I came to see you. You were mighty good to me a month ago, and I wanted to thank you."

He didn't mention the fact that he was also a trifle homesick, but she understood without being told. For an hour she sat and chatted with him, not talking about the *Saratoga* but about his father and mother, his home and the quiet woods and marshes of the Mullica.

He felt happier when he left, promising to return the next time the ship was in port.

Gid reached the wharf about sundown and found several other officers and men waiting for a boat to take them aboard. Among them was John Garvin, the Master.

"Well, young man," he remarked to Gid, "you'll see some sailing from now on." He rubbed his big hands with satisfaction. "Today," he explained, "we got our ballast. Eight tons o' pig iron out o' one o' the row galleys they use for harbor defense. It's all stowed in the hold now, and I'll warrant it'll make a world o' difference."

Gid hoped fervently that he was right. It was time, he felt, for someone—preferably his own ship—to strike a blow for liberty. In the taverns and on the streets of Philadelphia he had heard a lot of gloomy talk that day.

Down in the Carolinas General Gates had suffered one defeat after another and the South was now given up for lost. The British grip on New York seemed firmer than ever. Washington's army held North Jersey and most of the Hudson, but it was a weak and poorly equipped force. Any attack on Manhattan was out of the question.

Meanwhile the French fleet remained bottled up in Narragansett Bay, made helpless by a strong blockade of British warships. And there were rumors that a still more powerful fleet, under command of the famous Admiral Rodney, was on its way northward from the West Indies. Gid's spine tingled at the thought of a possible meeting with those fast British frigates and mighty ships-of-the-line.

If John Young had heard the reports, he gave no sign that they disturbed him. That evening and the next day he went about his preparations for another voyage with calmness and efficiency. Now that he had ballast, provisions and ammunition, he was eager to get to sea.

Some of the prisoners from the *Sarah* had volunteered to join the crew. A few others, who could not be won over to the American cause, were left in jail in Chester. After only four days in port the *Saratoga's* sails were hoisted and she moved down the Delaware on September 17. Next morning she cleared the Capes, heading north along the Jersey coast. It had been the Board of Admiralty's idea that the sloop-of-war should join forces with the two Continental frigates, the *Trumbull* and the *Deane*. But at the Delaware port of Lewes there had been no word of their whereabouts, and Captain Young was in no mood to hang around and wait for them.

Half a day's sailing proved that the added ballast had cured the ship's crankiness. They tried her before the wind, reaching and tacking, and she answered her helm perfectly, slicing through the water with all the speed her designers had expected of her.

Meanwhile the gun crews were drilled harder than ever. Young gave them his personal attention, moving from one cannon to the next, advising and reprimanding. Often he held the watch himself to time the drill. From now on there would be no excuse for poor marksmanship.

Warm weather and the brief stay in port had helped Anthony Castoff regain a little of his strength. Dr. Brown looked him over once or twice, shrugged his shoulders and admitted there was little a surgeon's skill could do for the man. However, the long, hard days at the gun didn't

seem to make him worse, and he did less complaining than some of the able-bodied seamen.

For a week they cruised along the New Jersey coast, sometimes in sight of land. Strangely they didn't sight a single sail in all that time. Finally, on the 25th, when the bluffs of the Jersey Highlands were a low-lying smudge on the horizon off the port bow, the topsail of a sloop was reported by the lookout. The vessel was well inshore, making all speed to reach the safety of Sandy Hook.

Young ordered more sail and the *Saratoga* went after her prey like a swooping hawk. Within half an hour she had overhauled the slower moving craft. The Stars and Stripes were flying from the peak as she bore down on the sloop.

"Lay a four-pounder across her bows!" the captain snapped, and the order was passed to the fore-deck. The forward four-pounder was under the command of Sam Clarkson. He loaded and aimed with alacrity and the ball flew true, skipping through the waves a scant hundred feet from the vessel's blunt bowsprit.

The shot brought immediate results. They could see men scurrying to haul the main sheet and bring the sloop into the wind. A scant five minutes later a boarding party was sent to take possession of the sloop.

Much to Gid's delight he was detailed to the longboat for this duty, as second in command to one of the master's mates. He primed his pistol and gripped his cutlass firmly as they swept alongside, but there was no show of resistance. The sloop, it turned out, was the *Elizabeth*, formerly of American registry. She had been captured a week or two earlier in the Chesapeake by a British privateer and was now on her way to New York, manned by a small prize crew.

Gid was in charge of the longboat when it returned to the *Saratoga* with the prisoners. He reported at once to the quarter-deck and answered the captain's questions.

The *Elizabeth* was a less valuable prize than the snow

had been. Her cargo consisted largely of new spars, taken from a half-built brig by the same privateer that had captured her. However, she would bring a few thousand dollars, and Young gave orders to the half dozen men left aboard as a prize crew to sail her immediately to Philadelphia.

The *Saratoga* hovered watchfully near until the captured vessel was within sight of Cape May, then headed out to sea once more. The weather stayed fair and the equinoctial storms that might be expected in late September failed to materialize. Day after day the lookouts in the fore and main tops stared across blue water unbroken by a speck of sail. But nobody in the ship had time to be bored.

Captain Young kept all hands busy with continued gun drills and exercises in seamanship. Sometimes Gid wondered if any crew under the new country's flag could be as thoroughly ready for battle as this one.

The men were keen as their cutlasses, honed to a razor edge. Daily they swarmed on deck, eagerly scanning the horizon. Some cursed the British for cowards. Others gave vent to their energies by racing each other up the ratlines or trying to beat the time of rival gun crews. Such competition was encouraged by the officers, and as a result they had a smart and happy ship.

In the first week of October the weather began to change. For two days the sky was dark and overcast and a long, sullen ground swell foreboded trouble. John Garvin, the Master, knew the signs. On his advice the *Saratoga* sailed eastward to gain plenty of sea room. Then, toward midnight of the sixth, the gale was upon them.

With the first fierce rush of wind out of the northeast, the topmen were sent scurrying aloft. Sail had already been shortened and inside of two minutes all the canvas was furled except a small storm jib. By the time the men regained the deck it was blowing a full gale.

Gid had never been at sea in a hurricane before and it was a wild experience. With hatches battened down and guns double-lashed, the sloop-of-war ran southward before the wind under bare poles. Well-ballasted now, she handled magnificently. Yet her decks were constantly awash from breaking seas and it was only by holding to the handlines, stretching from mast to mast, that a man could make his way forward or aft.

Wet to the skin, Gid went below at midnight. He poured the water out of his sea-boots and crawled into his bunk without undressing. With a blanket pulled around him he tried to let his own body heat dry some of the moisture out of his clothes. Usually, when he turned in at the end of the first night watch, he went to sleep at once. But tonight the strange, surging motion of the ship and the constant groan and creak of her timbers kept him awake.

He could feel the giddy rush of speed as she plunged down the slope of a great wave. Then, when the crest passed under, there would come a sickening moment of hesitation and a shaking of the oaken hull as she slipped back into the trough. And all the while she pitched—first her bow, then her stern pointing skyward.

Gid had heard of bigger vessels than the *Saratoga* being pooped by a monster sea in a storm like this. He wondered how it would feel to be buried deep under countless tons of water, or worse still what would happen if the ship broached to. So he lay there shivering until at last fatigue overcame his too vivid imagination.

At four in the morning, when he was roughly shaken back into consciousness by a heartless bosun's mate, he discovered they were still afloat. Pulling on his boots he gulped a pannikin of hot tea which the cook had somehow managed to brew in the water-logged galley, then stumbled topside.

The gale seemed to be blowing as hard as ever. And in the darkness the white-crested seas that loomed higher than the mizzen mast were terrible to behold. There was little for the watch on deck to do. They huddled miserably in any spot that offered a bit of shelter.

By noon on that memorable seventh of October, the storm had blown itself out. Tremendous seas were still running, but the clouds overhead broke into ragged patches of gray. It was even possible for Garvin and Faggo to take an observation and come fairly close to the ship's position.

They found the gale had blown them southwestward a full one hundred and fifty miles and they were now about ten leagues east by south of Cape Henry. Captain Young ordered the helm put about. If the bad weather returned he didn't want to be caught too close to Cape Hatteras. Also the long absence of any shipping along the coast to the northward was bound to be broken soon. The British needed supplies in New York and they could only get them by sea.

The *Saratoga* had sustained very little damage during

the storm. They examined her thoroughly that afternoon and found a few minor leaks that could be stopped with oakum. The bowsprit had also been cracked when the storm jib had blown out early in the gale. It was a simple matter for the carpenter to fish the bowsprit with a spare spar, and then the ship was as seaworthy as ever.

The morning of the eighth dawned gray and cloudy with the sea rough and the wind strong enough for reefed canvas. Up in the fore top Gid was bundled in his heavy jacket, keeping lookout and slapping his hands to warm them.

Over the port bow in the northwest quarter he thought he saw a momentary gleam of white on the edge of the steel-colored sea. He gripped a stay and leaned forward, his eyes glued to the spot. When it came again, he was sure.

"Sail ho!" he cried. "Three points off the bow to port. Wait! Now I think—yes—there's two of 'em!"

LIEUTENANT BARNEY himself came hurrying aloft at the call. He carried his telescope and was soon perched beside Gid, looking at the distant specks of sail.

"One's a full-rigger and a big one," he murmured. "Could be a frigate—even a ship o' the line. The little fellow's a sloop. Both bound north."

The *Saratoga* cracked on more sail and began pulling up on the other vessels hand over hand. Running on a beam wind she was heeled far to port, and Gid could look straight down from the swaying mast into the creaming seas below.

Inside an hour they were near enough to make out more of the two craft they were pursuing. As the larger ship's hull came up over the horizon Barney could see her gun ports through the glass.

"Whew!" he whistled. "Eleven ports on a side! But she's too big an' clumsy for a Navy cruiser. Must be a letter-o'-marque ship. She's flying the enemy flag."

After he returned to the deck Gid was also called down.

Quietly the word was passed to clear for action. When Gid glanced aloft he was surprised to see the British Union Jack whipping from the peak. Aaron Mathis saw his troubled look and grinned at him.

"That's allowed under the rules o' war," he said. "Gives us a chance to get in close. Been better if we'd done it when we tackled the *Keppel*. Only thing is, you've got to show your true colors when the fightin' starts."

Gid and his gun crew took their stations in the port battery while Barney was mustering some fifty armed seamen and marines amidships. By his order they crouched out of sight behind the bulwarks.

Swiftly the *Saratoga* raced up astern and cut between the two vessels, with the ship to starboard and the sloop some distance off to port. She was running so close that the British skipper must have been worried about a collision.

"What ship is that?" he hailed them through the speaking trumpet.

"The Continental sloop-of-war *Saratoga*," Young answered. "Heave to at once or I'll sink you!"

With his first words the Union Jack came down and the American flag was quickly hoisted. They were nearly abeam now and Captain Young ordered the starboard battery to open fire. The eight nine-pounders roared out with one voice, their round shot splintering the timbers of the big merchantman. Then, while the heavy cloud of smoke concealed their movements, the *Saratoga's* helm was put hard over to starboard.

In an instant they were alongside. There were men on

the yard arms with grappling hooks and they had been practicing for this moment. The irons shot out to catch the running gear of the ship as the two hulls ground together.

Gid heard a triumphant yell from Lieutenant Barney's crew of boarders. They jumped out from their hiding places and swarmed up and over the higher bulwark of the ship. The British officers made a hasty attempt to rally their men and a few stout-hearted tars fought doggedly. But the slashing Yankee attack swept all before it. The brief, bloody battle was over in a matter of minutes, and with half a dozen wounded lying on the reddened deck the captain surrendered.

The ship was the *Charming Molly*, commanded by Captain Robert Gill. She was sailing under a letter-of-marque, heavily armed for a merchantman. And her cargo —rum and sugar out of Jamaica for New York—was a rich prize indeed.

There was no time to lose if the *Saratoga* wanted to overtake the fleeing sloop. Young transferred the whole ship's company of ninety men, including several wounded, to the hold of his own vessel, left Barney aboard with a small prize crew, and immediately hauled the yards to give chase to his other quarry.

The sloop was now nearly hull down to leeward. However, she was no match for the fast-sailing American fighting ship. By late afternoon the *Saratoga* drew abeam and the sloop's flag was hauled down without a shot being fired. They found on boarding her that she was the *Two Brothers*. Her captain's name was Deane, and like her larger consort she was carrying rum and sugar.

As dusk fell they completed the business of bringing the British crew over to the sloop-of-war and five men were detailed to sail the prize north to the Delaware. Gid watched her till her upper canvas was lost in the darkness.

The *Saratoga* was cruising slowly northward that night when her crew heard the dull boom of a distant cannon. It was repeated exactly a minute later and the listeners knew it came from somewhere astern.

"That's a minute gun—a signal from a ship in trouble," Bill Faggo commented. "Reckon Lieutenant Barney must be trying to call us back."

The captain interpreted the sound the same way. When the third report sounded he had the ship put about at once and sent double lookouts into the tops. Two hours later they sighted a ship's lights. It was the *Charming Molly,* moving slowly toward them under shortened sail.

When he was within hailing distance, Captain Young hove to.

"Ahoy, there," he called. "Was that a distress signal?"

It was Barney who answered. "Aye, sir, your marksmanship was too good. We're hulled, right between wind an' water and we're taking it in faster'n we can pump. There's five feet in the hold now."

The sloop-of-war stood by while the carpenter was rowed over to the ship. Working in the dark of the hold and below the water line it took him several hours to plug the hole where the round shot had entered. Finally, just before dawn, he returned.

"She'll still leak some," he told the captain, "but they

ought to be able to keep on top of it with the pumps. There's some damage aloft, too—spars an' riggin'."

Young hailed Barney again. "Better not try for Philadelphia," he advised. "She's too badly crippled. Take her into the Chesapeake instead. That's only a dozen leagues or so, and I think you can make it."

They waved farewell and the larger ship, short-handed and barely seaworthy, put about for the Virginia Capes. Young must have hated to send her off alone, but he had other business on his mind now. During the night the prisoners had been questioned. From the two British captains, Gill and Deane, the Yankee officers heard that still richer prizes were nearby.

The word spread fast among the afterguard. By daylight Gid and the other midshipmen knew that the vessels they had taken were only part of the Jamaica convoy. Somewhere within sailing distance they might expect to find a good-sized ship, heavily armed, and two brigs. The ship, like the smaller vessel they had taken earlier, was named the *Elizabeth*. According to the prisoners she carried a big crew and her batteries included twenty-eight nine-pounder and six-pounder guns. One of the brigs, the *Nancy*, was also ready for trouble. She was armed with fourteen four-pounders and had enough men to handle them. The other brig, called the *Phoenix*, carried only a few small guns.

Despite the odds that would be against them, nobody in the sloop-of-war felt any qualms about tackling the three ships if they could be found. True, in sheer gun power the *Saratoga* would be outclassed more than two to one. In addition her crew was considerably reduced because of the score or more of men sent off in prizes. Her first lieutenant was gone. And the prisoners in her hold outnumbered her own company. But none of these facts could shake the confidence of Captain Young and his men. They had had a taste of victory and they were eager for more.

Double lookouts were continued all that day. The weather was clear as a bell, and if there were sails any-where on the horizon they were sure to be sighted. Under a fine spread of canvas the trim fighting ship raced north-ward expecting to overtake the convoy at any moment.

When darkness fell and they still had sighted nothing, the captain ordered the ship put about. They were then only a few leagues from Cape Henlopen and it seemed possible they might have run past the slower-moving ves-sels. Through the night they sailed eastward without hurrying, keeping a sharp watch. And at dawn Young gave the helmsman a new course, this time toward the south.

That morning seemed extra long to the eager men of the *Saratoga*. Gid spent hours up in the bows, holding to a jib-stay and hungrily scanning the sea ahead. He had worked over his cannon the day before, cleaning and pol-ishing the good Batsto iron, greasing the turnscrew on the gun-carriage, raising and lowering the muzzle. There had been no chance to fire in the engagement with the *Charming Molly*, and he hoped for an opportunity to prove the port battery was every bit as good as the star-board. Barent Sebring, the oldest of the midshipmen, was in charge of the number four starboard gun and had been doing some understandable bragging. He went so far as to claim it was his shot that had caused the water-line damage to the captured ship.

Jack Livingston had shut him up promptly by mentioning the fact that hulling a prize was fine but sinking her was less desirable. Nevertheless, the taunts of the starboard gunners rankled. If there was going to be another fight, Gid wanted his nine-pounder to be in the thick of it.

The boy heard a light step behind him and turned to see the stooped, cadaverous figure of Anthony Castoff standing there.

The seaman started to speak but was interrupted by a fit of coughing that shook his gaunt body. At last he pulled a piece of rumpled paper from his inside pocket.

"For you," he croaked.

Gid took it and smoothed it out, wondering what kind of message the man had brought. To his surprise there was no writing on the sheet. Instead it bore a drawing of a stormy sea and a ship. The boy stared, fascinated by the picture. It was so real he could almost feel the deck heave beneath him. The ship was the *Saratoga*, perfectly drawn, to the last spar and halyard. She was surging down the slope of a precipitous wave, running under naked masts, with flecks of white scud flying past in the gale.

"Gosh!" Gid murmured. "The hurricane! You *are* an artist, sure enough! But where'd you get the paints?"

"I couldn't get the colors I like most," Castoff answered. "Red an' yellow an' green. All I had was lampblack an' some tallow I begged from the cook. That's why I had to make it somethin' gray an' stormy."

His voice broke up in another coughing spell and he

turned away quickly, before Gid had a chance to thank him. The boy folded the paper with care and put it safely in his pocket. He knew it was no ordinary picture. If he could keep it, it would always be a vivid reminder of the voyage.

It was close to noon when the foremast lookout hailed the deck and announced three sail, dead ahead. Drums rolled, beating to quarters. The men poured on deck as if they had been waiting for the order. Quietly and quickly they went about the business of clearing for action. If the three approaching ships proved to be the Jamaica convoy they knew they were in for a fight, and they welcomed it.

Soon the oncoming vessels were visible from the deck. The ship was in the middle, her lofty royals standing well above the upper canvas of the two brigs. They must have sighted the sloop-of-war before this but they appeared to have no fear of her. Not one of them changed course.

Gid looked upward, expecting to see the Union Jack at the peak. But to his surprise it was the Stars and Stripes that flew there. This time Captain Young was going into battle under his true colors, bold in the knowledge that he had a fighting ship. Others in the crew saw the flag and sent up a cheer as they closed on the enemy.

There was no hailing done this time. On both sides the flags were visible and the ships were ready for what might come. Young sailed the *Saratoga* straight into the narrow lane between the ship and the larger brig.

To Gid's delight the *Elizabeth* would be on their port side. He growled a word of warning to Pilkinton, Caligan

and Castoff, adjusted his gun to point-blank range and waited, slow-match in hand, for the signal to fire.

It came almost before he could draw another breath. He whipped the glowing punk to the touch-hole and his cannon roared out in unison with the others. At almost the same instant the enemy ship must have let go her broadside, for there was a crash of splintered bulwarks and a scream of shot overhead. Deafened by the thunder of the guns and staggered by the concussion, he kept his wits about him.

"Quick, now," he yelled. "Haul and swab! Get her reloaded!"

The men worked like lightning and finished none too soon. For before the smoke had cleared the *Saratoga's* helm had been jammed over to port. She was right astern of the ship now, her port battery in position to rake the decks of the big West Indiaman.

"Fire a port broadside!" Lieutenant Allison bellowed. The answering reports came more raggedly this time, but Gid's gun spoke among the first. He had it trained squarely on the transom of the *Elizabeth* and just as the smoke pall settled he had the thrill of seeing the cabin mullions shattered by his shot.

Again they were reloading, while the sloop-of-war swung about on another tack. The brig, hit by the starboard battery's first volley, was wallowing helplessly. Disregarding her, Young brought the *Saratoga* in abeam of the ship, and this time it was the starboard guns that bore on the enemy.

Their broadside was as deadly as the port battery's had

been. And though the *Elizabeth* returned their fire, her disorganized gunners could do little damage. Most of her shots passed through the American's sails and shrouds. There was no doubt now that the three broadsides had done their work. Before the *Saratoga* could come about and descend on her again, the British ensign was hauled jerkily down and Young ordered the port battery to hold its fire. The whole engagement had been fought in a few minutes—one of the quickest victories in the annals of the young Continental Navy.

Off to the eastward they could see the other brig, the *Phoenix*, already hull-down and making all speed to get away. It would have been easy enough to overtake her, but with the two prizes already captured, the *Saratoga* had her hands full. She had won what was perhaps the most brilliant engagement fought by any ship in the Revolution.

IT WOULD BE HARD to imagine a more jubilant bunch of youngsters than the *Saratoga's* midshipmen that afternoon of October tenth. Barent Sebring was boasting again.

"I guess you saw," he said, "that after *we* fired the ship surrendered?"

"Sure," Gid told him with a laugh. "She was done for already. I'll wager we made sixteen clean hits in sixteen shots. Her skipper was smart enough to strike his colors before the port battery could hit him a third time."

"Well, we took her anyhow," said Jack Livingston. "I'd like to trade places with Sam, the lucky dog! He'll probably be home long before we are, and he'll be sailing up the Delaware as mate of a fine tall ship, to boot."

Gid also felt a twinge of envy, though Clarkson was one of his best friends. Almost before the smoke had cleared away Young had sent Master's Mate John Hackett aboard the *Elizabeth* as prizemaster and Sam Clarkson as his second in command. With them went forty of the *Saratoga's* remaining hands.

In the first boatload of prisoners that returned was David Taylor, the ship's captain. In reply to a few courteous questions he admitted that the *Elizabeth* had twenty-eight guns and a crew of a hundred men besides several passengers. Her cargo of rum and sugar was a big and valuable one.

The next boat brought more than a dozen badly wounded men, casualties of the port battery's raking fire. Dr. Brown and the surgeon from the ship were kept busy that afternoon dressing their wounds, and two of them died in spite of all that could be done for them.

Meanwhile the *Saratoga* headed westward to the place where the brig *Nancy* lay hove to. She had suffered considerable damage aloft, and though she didn't seem to be taking water, her skipper, Captain Oswald Eve, had watched the capture of the ship and decided it was safest to surrender. He was brought aboard, together with thirty hands and a few passengers. The cargo, he reported, was much the same as in the other prizes. John Garvin, the Sailing Master, was put in command of the prize crew, necessary repairs were made to the rigging, and shortly after sunset the brig set sail for the Delaware.

With a fine day's work completed, the crew of the *Saratoga* expected to follow her at once. But just as the sloop-of-war squared away, there came a boom of signal guns from the *Elizabeth*. She was coming up slowly astern of them.

Scowling at the delay, Young gave orders to back the yards and waited for the ship to approach within hailing distance. Soon they could hear Hackett's rather plaintive voice coming over the water.

"She sails very loggish," he announced. "And no wonder. Look how low she lies. There's holes down there as big as a man's head. We tried to pump her but she's got eight foot of water in her hold!"

Exasperated, the captain dispatched the carpenter with plugs to stop the holes and at the same time sent the other master's mate, Bill Faggo, to take over the command in Hackett's place. They stood by then until the carpenter's return and finally made sail about midnight.

Gid stood a trick at the wheel that night, for the *Saratoga's* crew had shrunk to half its original numbers and every man was needed. The course was due north and the breeze fair. By the end of the watch the sloop-of-war was in home waters once more, only a few leagues south and east of Cape Henlopen. The boy turned in at four o'clock and went to sleep with the happy thought that when his watch was called again they would be well into Delaware Bay.

He woke to the furious shrilling of the bosun's pipes and groped in the darkness for his boots. Surely eight bells couldn't have struck so soon. Then he heard the order bawled loudly down the hatch.

"All hands out! Take battle stations!"

Still in a half stupor of fatigue he scrambled up into the gray light of a cloudy daybreak. Two sails had been sighted a few minutes earlier and now the deck was being cleared for action.

*　　*　　*

Not an American aboard, including the bold Captain Young, knew what had been happening along the seaboard since they had started their cruise. Actually it was little short of a miracle that the *Saratoga* was still afloat, considering the weight of ships and guns against her.

The rumors about Admiral Rodney had been all too true. Out of New York, on October 2, had sailed a formidable British squadron with orders to sweep every Yankee from the seas. There were four great ships-of-the-line, the *Triumph*, the *Terrible*, the *Alcide* and the *Intrepid*. And with them were five frigates, the *Cyclops*, the *Boreas*, the *Greyhound*, the *Iris* and the *Raleigh*—all twice as heavily armed as the little American sloop-of-war.

In addition to these nine ships, Rodney had detached four other frigates from the main fleet on his way north from the West Indies. Two of them were cruising off the Carolinas and another pair patrolled the entrance to the Chesapeake.

Only by the purest luck had the *Saratoga* missed an early encounter with the squadron coming from New York. It was the threat of the coming storm that had sent her off to the eastward on the very day Rodney's ships had cleared Sandy Hook.

That same hurricane that drove the sloop-of-war so far south had played havoc with the British squadron. The seventy-four gun *Terrible* and the *Cyclops* both had their mizzen masts carried away and went limping back to port after the storm. And the frigates *Triton* and *Guadaloupe*, cruising in southern waters, were so badly battered that they, too, had to make for New York. It was only by heaving eight of her cannon overboard that the *Guadaloupe* managed to stay afloat.

Even so there were still nine big fighting ships of King George's Navy prowling the coast, and the *Saratoga*, heading for the Delaware, was right in the midst of them.

Perhaps John Young had a presentiment of danger. At any rate he advanced with more caution this time, and kept the spyglass shifting from one sail to the other. At about seven o'clock he turned suddenly to Lieutenant Allison. From where Gid stood by the breach of his gun he could hear what the captain said.

"That vessel dead ahead of us," he told the younger officer, "looks to me like a merchant brig. Now take a look at the other one, over there to the northwest. What do you make of her?"

Allison put the glass to his eye and leveled it on the distant sail. When he answered, he seemed to hesitate.

"Well," he said at last, "maybe I'm crazy, sir, but— I'd say she was a ship-o'-the-line!"

Young nodded. "Right," he replied heartily. "A seventy-four, unless I'm much mistaken. But they're a couple of leagues apart, and I'm going to snatch that brig right under the big fellow's nose. Give the order to crack on every stitch of canvas we can carry!"

With all her sails set and drawing, the sloop-of-war raced down on her intended prey, white water streaming from under her forefoot. The brig saw her coming and quite possibly made out the flag at her peak. In haste she veered to starboard, away from the protection of the larger ship, and tried to run eastward before the wind. Immediately Captain Young changed course to cut her off.

They overhauled the fleeing vessel in a burst of furious sailing, and the captain hailed her from within easy cannon shot.

"Heave to," he shouted, "or I'll sink you. What brig is that?"

The other ship hauled down her ensign and came promptly into the wind.

"We surrender," a boyish voice replied. "This is the brig *Providence*, a British prize. We're bound for New York."

Young was so shorthanded now that finding an officer to command still another prize was a problem. He frowned as he looked at the handful of men on deck. Gid straightened his shoulders and tried to act like officer material, but the captain's eye went past him toward the big ship-of-the-line, now bearing down on them under a tower of white canvas.

"Penfield!" he barked. "Pick six men and get over to the brig. You'll have to work fast or that man-o'-war'll be on our heels."

Midshipman Nat Penfield jumped to obey. He had a boat over in a jiffy and quickly sent the British prize crew back aboard the *Saratoga*. Before the boat was hoisted in, the brig was scudding off to the eastward, away from land.

Captain Young ordered a course to the north, with the

wind abeam. Meanwhile the prisoners from the *Providence* were lined up under the break of the poop.

"Which of you was in command?" the captain asked, and a pink-cheeked lad of sixteen or so took a smart step forward.

"I was, sir," he announced proudly. "Midshipman William Thackstone, of his Majesty's frigate *Triton.*"

Young nodded, trying to suppress a smile. "And can you tell me what ship that is, Mr. Thackstone?" he asked, pointing at the approaching man-of-war.

"Yes, sir. His Majesty's ship-of-the-line *Alcide,* seventy-four guns," was the reply.

"Thank you. Mr. Jones, show the other prisoners to their quarters below. I'd like to talk further with the midshipman."

Gid escorted the seven members of the prize crew down to join the two hundred odd men already in the hold. It was a nervous job for he knew the prisoners now outnumbered the ship's company by four to one. However, he got the men from the brig safely stowed away without any sign of an uprising, and hurried back to his gun.

Young Thackstone's piping voice came to him clearly, as he answered the captain's questions. The *Providence,* he said, was a Yankee merchant brig with a cargo of sugar and coffee out of Port au Prince for Philadelphia. She had been captured by the *Triton* and the *Guadaloupe* southeast of the Virginia Capes, and Thackstone was sent aboard with a small crew to take her into New York.

When the youth had been sent below with the other prisoners, John Young continued to pace the quarter-deck, his eye on the big British vessel. As soon as it became apparent that she did not mean to change course, he ordered the *Saratoga's* helm put over. Warily he edged closer, keeping just out of range of those heavy guns. The sloop-of-war darted in, then sheered off, trying to draw the *Alcide's* attention away from the fleeing brig.

"Just like a hen partridge," Tom Pilkinton remarked with a chuckle. "You know, sir—when she's protectin' her chicks." And Gid agreed. He had seen a mother bird flutter around a hunter, pretending her wing was broken, and Young's tactics were much the same. But unfortunately the effort was in vain.

The British captain had witnessed a sample of the *Saratoga's* speed and must have known she could sail circles around him. The *Providence*, on the other hand, had no such advantage. Gid watched the huge fighting ship gain on her slowly but surely and his heart was heavy.

Nothing could save poor Nat Penfield and his seamen now. He remembered how eagerly the lad had gone over the side to take his first command, and how he had envied him the chance. Gid breathed a prayer that nothing worse than capture might happen to his fellow midshipman.

After an hour of fruitless maneuvering Captain Young gave up the idea of decoying the *Alcide* away from her quarry. Gloomily he turned the *Saratoga's* bow westward and made for home.

*   *   *

Very early in the morning of the 14th of October the sloop-of-war dropped anchor at Chester. The state of the

121

tide made it impossible for her to reach Philadelphia that day. However, John Young had an urgent message to deliver in the city, and he picked out Midshipman Jones to carry it for him.

"You're a good rider," he told the boy, "and I want this letter put in Francis Lewis's hands by noon. Here's money. Hire yourself the best horse they've got at the inn stable. Tell 'em it's Navy business and I'll guarantee the nag's return. You should find Mr. Lewis at the office of the Board of Admiralty, on Front Street, once you've reached Philadelphia."

Gid shook out his dress uniform, hurried ashore and went at once to the inn near the waterfront. Captain Young's name impressed the landlord. Within ten minutes the boy was astride a rangy gray horse, cantering up the dusty road that wound along the shore of the Delaware.

Once he passed an orchard where ruddy windfallen apples lay in the grass. Dismounting quickly, he helped himself to three or four, gave one to the horse and was on his way again. After a month of sea rations the sweet, tangy fruit tasted more delicious than anything he could remember.

At the hamlet of Darby he stopped once more for bread and cheese, washed down with water that was fresh and sparkling—far different from the scummy fluid in the ship's butts. And at last, after thirty weary miles, he climbed down stiffly in front of William West's house, where the Board of Admiralty had its quarters. There was an iron hitching post at the edge of the flagged walk. He tied the reins to it, brushed some of the dust from his coat and climbed the steps to knock at the door.

A servant admitted him and led him at once to a ground floor room off the hallway. Inside he saw two men bent above a table that was cluttered with documents and letters. He recognized them as Commissioner Lewis and Secretary Brown. Both glanced up at the same time, frowning at the interruption. He thought Lewis looked worn and worried.

"Yes?" the commissioner asked irritably.

Gid saluted. "Midshipman Jones, sir," he said and held out the letter. "From Captain Young of the *Saratoga,* sir."

"The *Saratoga!*" Lewis exclaimed. "Good! Let me read it."

Little by little the lines of care disappeared from his face as he drank in the news Young had sent him. Seeing his delight Brown hurried around the table to read over his shoulder.

"Amazing!" Lewis murmured. "Six prizes! Three of them large merchantmen—and heavily armed. Two hundred and twenty prisoners in the hold! Gad, Brown—it's well we got that new jail built. Get off a letter at once to the jail-keeper, and another to Young. Tell him to send us a full list of the prisoners' names and ranks, and a report on any repairs and supplies he needs. We can't afford to let the sloop-of-war hang around in port. This fellow Young is one captain who shows results!"

He swung about and held out his hand to Gid. "Young man," he said, "you've done well indeed to bring us this packet of news! Here, Jackson—fetch a glass of Madeira for the young gentleman.”

Gid bowed. “Never mind the wine, sir,” he stammered. “But if there’s milk in the house I’d like a glass of that. We don’t keep a cow on the *Saratoga*.”

Francis Lewis had good reason to rejoice over Young's triumphant return. The frigates *Trumbull* and *Deane* had sailed up the river after three weeks of cruising and reported no prizes worth mentioning. They had taken two small coasting vessels with little of value in their cargo, and one of these had probably been recaptured since it was long overdue.

As usual there was no money available to get the frigates refitted for sea. The Continental Congress had all it could do to supply Washington's army in meager fashion. And funds for naval warfare would have to come from such prizes as could be taken.

While Secretary Brown's quill pen scratched busily over the paper, Lewis asked Gid a hundred questions about details of the cruise. He reveled in the boy's account of the *Saratoga's* new sailing qualities. And he wanted to hear everything possible about their victory over the bigger and better armed *Elizabeth*.

"You must have been short of officers before the voyage

was done," he observed. "Let us hope they all bring their prizes safe home."

"I'm afraid that's impossible, sir," Gid answered sadly. "The last we saw of the *Providence* she was being overhauled by the *Alcide*. And it was too early in the day for darkness to save her. Nat Penfield was in command and I fear he's a prisoner now."

Lewis nodded soberly. "Too bad," he said. "I'll have the painful duty of telling his parents. But he shouldn't be long in captivity. We've plenty of prisoners to exchange at last."

One of the last orders Captain Young had given Gid was to return to his ship as soon as he was able, after delivering the letter to Lewis and another note to Mistress Young. "I doubt you'll make it today," he had said, "for the horse must rest. But if my wife is at home she'll be happy to put you up for the night."

Some time toward mid-afternoon the boy rode down to the captain's house on Laurel Street. The small Negro lad, Favorite, came and took his horse to the stable. And Mistress Young welcomed him with joy when she heard of her husband's safe return.

Once more Gid was called upon to tell the story of the cruise from beginning to end. After an excellent supper he was shown to a pretty guest room where the unaccustomed softness of the featherbed kept him awake half the night.

Shortly after breakfast he mounted the hired gray and rode out of the city toward Chester.

John Young had already received the message from Lewis and was in high spirits when Gid reached the *Saratoga*. He inquired after his wife's health and clapped the boy on the shoulder.

"You've done well, Mr. Jones," he said with a smile. "There'll be ample reward for all of us, I hope, when the prizes come in. Those three bigger vessels and their cargoes ought to bring a tidy sum, and half of it goes to the officers and crew. I'll need you aboard for a few days, till we get our prisoners disposed of. Then the ship will probably have to be docked at Philadelphia for repairs and I expect you'll be able to go home on leave."

That afternoon boatload after boatload of British tars were set ashore under guard. A militia company in Chester undertook to march them up to Philadelphia, where Thomas Bradford, Deputy Commissioner of Prisoners, was ready to receive them in his new jail.

After all the prisoners were gone, Captain Young set the crew to cleaning out the hold and taking stock of the damages to the ship. There were a good many places where she had received minor injuries in the hurricane and her various fights. Most of the coaming around one of the hatches had been smashed by a cannon ball. In several other places shot had crashed through the stout pine sheathing. One boat was badly stove and many of the chocks had been shot away or carried away by the gale winds of early October. More important, a fair amount of studding had to be replaced, and the jury job done on the bowsprit would hardly hold through another storm.

The Navy Board sent inspectors down to look the sloop-of-war over and report on her condition. Much to Young's regret he had to agree with them that the *Saratoga* should be put in the repair dock at Mr. Humphreys' yard in Philadelphia. The captain had held some hope that he might replenish his supplies, recruit a few seamen and get to sea again. Now he had no choice but to take the ship upriver.

With the first lieutenant, sailing master and both master's mates off on prizes, Gid and the other remaining midshipmen were temporarily berthed in the officers' quarters aft. The cabins were tiny enough, but the move gave them a sense of importance. Also the meals were considerably better and they were able to listen to the talk of the afterguard.

Much of that talk was about the vessels they had taken, and the prize crews aboard them. As the days passed and the *Charming Molly*, the ship *Elizabeth* and the brig *Nancy* were still unreported, John Young began to grow anxious.

"There's been no really bad weather to set them off their course," he grumbled. "And every one of 'em's under command of an experienced man. The *Elizabeth's* crew's big enough so she might even do some fighting if she had to."

"Well, sir," Lieutenant Allison replied, trying to cheer him, "you know how it goes at sea. They had to get used to their ships first of all. Head winds could have set them back, or they're still having trouble with those leaks. They'll be sighted soon, never fear. I wouldn't wonder if they were sailing up from Lewes this very minute. I wish I could say as much for the *Providence,* but I guess she's gone."

After a delay of several days the *Saratoga* was piloted through the chevaux-de-frise and reached the Southwark docks. It was the last week of October when they turned her over to her famous builder, Joshua Humphreys.

Gid drew his pay that afternoon. It wasn't a very large sum, even in Continental dollars, but at least he had money in his pocket. Jack Livingston accompanied him ashore and they got a room together at an inn for the night. The fate of their friends in the prizes was much on both their minds, and they asked for news as soon as they were ashore.

"You know," Gid told his companion, "the *Elizabeth* had orders to head for the Chesapeake. Sam Clarkson would want to let his folks know, soon as he could. Anyhow the ship should have been reported from Baltimore by this time."

Eagerly they purchased copies of the *General Advertiser* and the *Pennsylvania Gazette,* scanning the advertisements, news notices and reports on the progress of the war. There was nothing about the arrival of the missing prizes, but plenty about the cruise of the *Saratoga.*

"We seem to be famous," Jack laughed. "Listen to this in the *Advertiser:*

" 'On Wednesday the 18th instant, arrived, after a short cruise, the *Saratoga* sloop-of-war, commanded by the gallant Captain John Young. On the 30th of September he retook the sloop *Elizabeth;* and on the 8th of October fell in with the ship *Charming Molly*, of 22 guns, Captain Gill, who, after a smart engagement, struck.

" 'On the 9th Captain Young took the brig *Nancy*, of fourteen 4-pounders, commanded by Oswald Eve, in company with the ship *Elizabeth*, of 28 6 and 9 pounders, Captain Gill'—they got that wrong. 'Twas Captain Taylor in the *Elizabeth*—'Captain Gill, who, after a sharp conflict of two glasses (in which, as in the former action, the greatest bravery and good conduct was displayed by the worthy commander of the *Saratoga*) struck, being much damaged in her hull and rigging, and having six feet of water in her hold. The last three vessels were from Jamaica, bound to New York, having on board valuable cargoes of rum, sugar, &c.

" 'To this well merited success of Captain Young, his Officers and Men, we must add the re-capture of the sloop *Providence*, of this port, late prize of the *Triton* and *Guadaloupe* frigates.

" 'We hourly expect the arrival of the above prizes in this port, two of them, it is said, having already entered the Delaware.' "

He was glad to pause for breath after reading the long sentences. Gid chuckled.

"Mighty sweet words," he said. "They haven't had too many successful fights to report, so they went overboard on us. What was that about the *Elizabeth*—'after a sharp conflict of two glasses'? That would be an hour. Didn't seem to me it took that long."

"No," said Jack. "You're right. We only had to fire

three good broadsides. I wish I was as sure as the editors that those prizes would turn up. The two they mention must be the little sloop *Elizabeth* and the *Two Brothers*. Nothing at all about the big ones."

They ordered an excellent supper that night and after going to bed they talked awhile about their plans. A month's leave! It seemed time enough for almost anything they wanted to do.

"I'll spend a day or two with our friends, where my sisters are staying," Jack said. "Then I'd better go up to Trenton and let Father give me some more good advice. He's a wonderful old gentleman and I love him dearly, but he likes to warn me about the pitfalls a sailor is liable to tumble into. I expect you want to see your people down at Batsto. Why don't you come visit us in Trenton afterward?"

"I'd like to," Gid replied. "I'll have to see how things work out, but don't be surprised if you see me riding up to the governor's mansion."

They parted early next day. Gid found that the Egg Harbor coach would not be leaving till afternoon, so he wandered about the city, looking at the sights. It was down on Front Street, near the docks, that he ran into Aaron Mathis. The husky bosun's mate greeted him warmly.

"You waitin' for the coach, too?" he asked. "Good. We'll ride down together. Too bad about the prizes, isn't it?"

"What about them? You mean there's news?"

"Aye—bad news. I was down at Humphreys' yard a

bit ago an' heard it from Lieutenant Allison. Seems the *Providence* was taken by that big man-o'-war, just as we thought. She got to New York about the fifteenth. But then, a couple o' days later, two British frigates came up with the *Nancy* an' the *Charming Molly*. That means Garvin an' Lieutenant Barney an' Nat Penfield are all prisoners in the hulks by this time, along with their crews."

Gid was silent for a minute, saddened by the thought of his friends and what they might be suffering.

"Maybe they'll be exchanged," he said at last. "Some of 'em, any way. You know we took some prisoners, too."

Aaron looked doubtful. "The officers might be exchanged," he replied. "But what they do with seamen is different. They'll press most of 'em for their own ships or for privateers. I guess we can say good-bye to that big prize money."

"Oh, well," Gid tried to cheer him, "there's still the *Elizabeth*. She was the richest o' the lot. And with Faggo and Hackett both aboard, and a forty-man crew, she ought to be safe in Baltimore by now."

Aaron still appeared doubtful. "Hackett an' Faggo didn't jibe too well," he said. "I reckon Hackett's a better seaman but he's a bit timid-like. An' I'm pretty sure he'd resent it when the skipper sent Faggo to take over the command. With so many British cruisers out, the *Elizabeth's* goin' to need luck an' a good captain to get home."

They crossed the river by the ferry and boarded the stage at the Bull and Stars on the other shore. It was a cold, bumpy trip, for there had been a sharp frost the night before and the rutted road was frozen. Sleeping at an inn that night, they reached Egg Harbor the next afternoon and were lucky enough to get a ride to Batsto on a farmer's wagon. It was eight o'clock and pitch dark when they climbed down stiffly in front of the Jones house.

*　　*　　*

Gid found that a thirty-day leave was a great deal shorter than he had thought it would be when it started. Aaron went on downriver after spending the first night with him. But he had many other friends in the village to see, and of course his father and mother could never get enough of his company. He told all about his life aboard the *Saratoga*, not once but several times.

As far as his mother was concerned, she wanted to hear about the food, the sleeping quarters and the opportunities for bathing and washing clothes. Battles were less to her liking. It was only when he was alone with his father that he could recount the more dangerous and exciting parts of his two voyages.

"And how did you find the guns?" asked Reuben Jones. "All sound and true, I hope."

Gid laughed. "Best guns in the Continental Navy!" he assured the ironmaster. "And the best served, too. Not even John Paul Jones ever had better gun-crews than ours. Why, we finished a ship with near double our weight of metal in just three broadsides! Left her so full of holes the prize crew had trouble keeping her afloat."

He paused suddenly, and the animation left his face.

"What's the matter, son?" his father asked.

"Just wondering if they did keep her afloat. She hadn't

133

been reported when I left the city. One o' my best friends was in her—Sam Clarkson. I wrote home about a party we had at his place, back in August."

Toward the middle of November, when Gid had been at home two weeks, a letter came for him. It was from Jack Livingston, saying that his father had not been well and that he now expected to leave shortly for Philadelphia.

"By the way," he added in a postscript, "you will be as sorry as I to hear of the capture of our prize *Elizabeth*. Father got a packet of news smuggled out of New York. Rivington's newspaper, the *Royal Gazette*, reports she was taken on October 19th by the British sloop-of-war *Swift*. Poor Sam! We must hope for his early exchange."

Gid saddled his mare next morning and rode down the winding road to Aaron's home at Lower Bank. The marshes were gray-brown now and the leafless maples and gum trees lifted naked arms against the November sky. He saw great flocks of ducks and brant flying over. On the lower river a few oyster boats were at work, but otherwise he sighted no people until he reached the little village.

Mrs. Mathis was in her backyard, hanging up clothes to dry in the sharp wind that came from the sea. Gid tethered Blossom to a post and went around the house to speak to her.

"You lookin' for Aaron?" she asked. "Oh, I guess you're the Jones boy he was with in the *Saratoga*. I'm sorry, Mr. Jones, but Aaron's off at sea. Sailed in the privateer *Absecon* last week."

"B-but," Gid stammered, "his leave's up in less than two weeks."

"Oh, don't let that worry ye," she laughed. "They're only out for a short cruise. I expect him back 'most any day now."

Gid was relieved. "Well," he said, "I had some news to give him, but it'll keep. Tell him I'll be looking for him at my house a couple of days before the twenty-fifth. That's when we have to get back to the ship."

13

Colonel Cox had been away at the time of Gid's home-coming. He returned to Batsto on November twentieth, and the next day the young midshipman put on his uniform and went to pay a call.

The good colonel, as red-faced and full of fire as ever, invited him into the parlor of the mansion at once. He pumped his hand with great energy and asked all about his life in the Navy.

Gid made the account as brief and as modest as he could, remembering to thank the gentleman for his letter of recommendation to Captain Young. As he talked he looked around the room, hoping for some indication that the colonel's niece had been there. It was foolish, he knew, for she was many miles away at school.

At last, as he was about to leave, Cox suddenly smacked his fist into his palm.

"By George!" he exclaimed. "I nearly forgot. Wasn't there a young fellow named Mathis in your ship—bosun's mate or something?"

"Yes, sir. He's a good friend of mine."

"I got a dispatch this morning," said the colonel. "It told of the capture of a privateer from the Mullica, somewhere down the coast. Mentioned Mathis as one o' the crew. Too bad, eh?"

Gid's face was pale. "It's worse than that, sir," he answered. "Aaron's leave is up in four days. He'll be listed as a deserter."

On the way home he thought sadly about his friend. Going out on the *Absecon* had been a lark for Aaron, he knew—a natural thing for a born sailor to do when he had time on his hands. But the officers of the *Saratoga* wouldn't look at it that way. The lad would be disgraced in a ship that was proud of its crew's record. And as for his chances of exchange, it seemed unlikely that the government would try to get him back from the British merely to clap him into a Continental prison.

Two days later Gid was on his way to Philadelphia once more. His eagerness to get to sea was dampened somewhat by the feeling that the *Saratoga* wouldn't be the same. Sam Clarkson was gone, and Nat Penfield, not to mention such fine officers as Barney and Garvin. And now Aaron, too.

He reached the city on the morning of the twenty-fifth. It was freezing weather with a light snow falling. Gid buttoned his reef-coat tightly, turned up the collar, and bent forward into the wind, carrying his seabag on his shoulder.

His way to the Southwark docks led past dingy warehouses, sailors' boarding places and grog shops. There were few people about in that weather. As he approached a

street corner he saw a man ahead of him moving slowly
and uncertainly. He thought little of it, for there were
always drunks along the waterfront. Gid had almost overtaken him when the man lurched to the side of a building
and leaned against the wall, his whole thin body shaken by
a hollow cough.

The boy took two or three steps past him, then paused
suddenly and turned, looking into the dark, tortured face
of Anthony Castoff.

The Negro returned his stare with dull eyes. There was
recognition in them but no hope.

"Yes, Mr. Jones," he breathed hoarsely. "It's me, or
what's left o' me."

Gid put out his hand. "Look," he said, filled with com-
passion, "you'll have to get back to the ship. Let me help
you."

Castoff shook his head. "It's no use, sir. Reckon I've
made my last voyage. They'd be givin' me sea burial, an'
I don't want that." He shuddered, his teeth chattering.
"So c-c-cold, an' dark an' deep!"

There was little the midshipman could say. Perhaps his
duty was to drag the man aboard, but he was still on leave
and not under naval discipline. He laid his hand gently
on the sick man's shoulder.

"I've still got your picture of the ship and the storm,"
he said. "My folks think it's wonderful."

Castoff's eyes brightened for a moment. "That's good,
sir. It's time you run along now an' I hope you get a better hand for the gun than me."

Gid said good-bye and went on his way.

From the wharf he hailed the *Saratoga*. She had left the repair dock and now lay at her mooring, half a cable's length from shore. Presently a boat put off and carried him and a few other returnees to the ship.

The officer of the deck was strange to him, but he saluted and reported himself back.

"Glad to see you aboard, Mr. Jones," said the young officer. "I'm your new second lieutenant. My name's James Pyne—from South Carolina."

He said the last words proudly. Gid liked his looks, for he had a bold, rugged face, weathered by wind and sun, and the crinkles at the corners of his eyes spoke of years at sea.

After stowing his dunnage the boy asked permission to speak to the captain. He found John Young in his cabin, deep in a pile of paper work. But he looked up with a hearty smile at Gid's entrance.

"Ah, Mr. Jones," he said. "Ready for another bout with the enemy?"

"Aye, sir," Gid responded with a grin. "I'm afraid I have a piece of bad news, though."

Haltingly he told what he knew about Aaron. "He was counting on coming back with me, I'm sure, sir, for he was as proud of serving on the *Saratoga* as I am. They only expected to be out for a week, and the cruise promised some adventure. Nobody could have foreseen it would end the way it did."

Captain Young's jaw set. "That's no excuse," he snapped. "We've got all the crew we need, but good warrant officers are harder to find. I had plans for that lad, and now his record's spoiled. If the report's true and he doesn't turn up today, he'll have to go down in the log as a deserter."

Gid saluted and left the cabin with a heavy heart. He was somewhat cheered toward evening when Jack Livingston came aboard. The New Jersey governor's son was in fine spirits.

"Did you hear," he said, "that Nat Penfield's been exchanged? The skipper swapped that young Britisher, Thackstone, for him. I'd say we got the best of the bargain."

Jack had been having a gay time with his Philadelphia friends. He told Gid about parties and balls he had attended, and brought one message that gave the boy a real lift.

"I saw a friend of yours at Nancy Breckinridge's," he said. "A mighty pretty little baggage she was, too. Peggy Lane—remember her? She said to tell you she was making you a gift and hoped we wouldn't sail before it's ready."

"Making it?" Gid replied, knowing his face was red. "What do you suppose it can be?"

Jack laughed. "Some feminine frippery or other, no doubt. Perhaps it's a bow of embroidered ribbon to wear over your heart. The girl thinks a good bit of you, I gathered. Too bad she had to go back to school. She and Nancy were only at home for a week."

The hands came straggling back that night and next morning a general muster was called amidships. All were present and accounted for but Aaron and one other. The name of Anthony Castoff was shouted three times with no reply. Then a squad of marines went ashore to look for him. Gid kept his mouth shut but he hoped the poor fellow would not be found.

The snow had stopped, but the sky stayed gray and cold. Three days passed and Nat Penfield came back to the *Saratoga.* He was thin and pale after a month in the prison ship in Wallabout Bay, but the experience hadn't broken his spirit.

"All I can say," he told his friends in the midshipmen's berth, "is don't get captured! The food is awful, even compared to ours. The hulks are cold, too, and there's only one filthy blanket for three men. You know the dirty lobsterbacks wouldn't exchange Barney or Garvin or Faggo or Hackett. All four of 'em were put aboard a ship for England a couple of weeks ago. They were in bad shape, too, and I suppose they'll just lie and rot in the jail at Plymouth."

The marines had come back empty-handed from their search for Castoff. After that the ordered routine of the ship went on as usual. Blaney Allison had been promoted to first lieutenant to fill Barney's shoes, and his first task was to hammer the new crew into shape. He worked them hard but there were very few lubbers in the group and the others quickly mastered their tasks. As a matter of fact, the *Saratoga's* reputation was such that good seamen chose to join her instead of the many privateers that thronged the river. Her lot was far better than that of the *Trumbull, Deane* and *Confederacy,* whose captains were constantly in hot water for impressing merchant seamen.

Time dragged by while they waited for money to be

raised, so that the ship might get her supplies of food and ammunition.

"Br-r-r!" growled Barent Sebring, threshing his arms to keep warm on night watch. "If the Admiralty Board doesn't give us help soon we're likely to be frozen in for the winter!"

It wasn't as improbable as it sounded, for many members of the crew could remember Januaries when the Delaware opposite the city was solid ice from bank to bank.

At last, in the second week of December, the victualers' barges came alongside, and powder and shot were delivered. Part of the ship's company was given a day's shore leave. Gid was not among the lucky ones, but when Jack Livingston returned that night he had a small parcel for him.

"That's right," he chuckled. "It's from the fair Peggy. She sent it to my sister Sue and asked that I be instructed to deliver it."

Gid fumbled at the cord and finally opened the package. Inside was a dark blue knitted cap of wool and a tiny note.

"Dear Mr. Midshipman Jones," it said. "As you will see, I am not expert at knitting but I made this with my own hands—every stitch. It's to keep you warm on winter nights when you are at the masthead or at the wheel— and thinking, I dare to hope, of your most humble servant, Peggy Lane."

He put the cap on with clumsy hands. It was warm and comfortable, a good fit. Before turning in he wrote her a letter of thanks.

The winter cruise of the *Saratoga* began on December fifteenth. It was a bleak day, with heavy fog over the river, and the pilot they took on to guide the ship through the twisting channel and the chevaux-de-frise had trouble finding his markers. More time was lost at Chester because of unfavorable wind and tides, and it was the morning of the eighteenth when they dropped anchor off Reedy Island.

A merchant fleet of considerable size was supposed to rendezvous there, and the sloop-of-war and the *Confederacy* were to convoy them south to Cuba and the Dutch West Indies. Through the mist they were just able to see the outline of a big frigate moored nearby.

Later that afternoon John Young was rowed over to talk to Captain Harding, in command of the *Confederacy*. The fog lifted a little and they could see some of the merchant fleet at anchor. By the time Young returned, several of the vessels' captains had come aboard to discuss the voyage with him.

"We're ready to sail early tomorrow," Gid heard him tell them. "Signals are arranged, so that Harding and I will know what we're doing. If you'll all keep well together we can promise you a good offing and a safe voyage."

There were thirteen ships in all, Gid learned, and they had valuable cargoes of flour and tobacco for Cap François, Havana and St. Eustatius.

The next day dawned fair with a good breeze. Young ran up the signal flags for departure and the fleet made sail. They made good headway down the bay for a couple of leagues, but then the wind failed and they all lay becalmed. At ten o'clock a fresh breeze filled the canvas again. It was from the northwest, blowing on their starboard quarter, and it grew stronger. Off Bombay Hook sharp squalls sent the hands hurrying aloft to reef topsails throughout the convoy.

To Captain Young's surprise and disgust the *Confederacy* signaled that her pilot didn't want to risk sailing farther in that weather. A moment later she swung head to wind and her cable ran clanking out as she came to anchor.

The half gale that was blowing didn't bother the *Saratoga*, and most of her charges were running merrily along down the bay. Young signaled Harding to follow as soon as possible and sped after the merchant fleet, of which he was now sole guardian.

It was toward evening when they sighted the lighthouse tower at Lewes, Delaware. There was a flag flying from the structure, telling them that the entrance to the bay was clear of hostile sails. The *Saratoga* cracked on more canvas and shepherded her flock out past Cape Henlopen in the gathering dusk.

THAT NIGHT when they cleared the Capes was the twentieth of December. Gid remembered because he had been on watch when the last glimpse of land vanished in the darkness, and he wondered where he would be on Christmas Day. Somewhere far to the south he hoped, in the edge of the warm Gulf Stream.

The wind held through the night, and they were well offshore when morning came. From the lookout post in the fore top Gid could count all thirteen sails of the convoy. They were well bunched and moving at a fair rate of speed.

That was too unusual to continue long. In every fleet of merchant ships there were some that were naturally fast sailers and some that were clumsily handled. By afternoon the convoy had begun to spread and straggle. The *Saratoga* was back among the laggard vessels, urging them forward, when a lookout hailed the deck.

"There's some sort o' flag signals on that ship way out to port," the man said. "I can't read 'em from here."

Lieutenant Pyne ran forward with a telescope and hurried up the ratlines. After a moment's scrutiny of the distant vessel he called down that they were signaling the presence of a strange sail, still over the horizon from the *Saratoga*.

At once Captain Young ordered a hoist of signals of his own. They told the convoy to get together and proceed on course. Then he called all hands to quarters and put the helm over to port.

Gid took his battle station, hoping for action. In the general shake-up for the new cruise he had been given a gun in the starboard battery. Tom Pilkinton was still a member of his crew, but Caligan had been taken prisoner in the *Elizabeth*, and Castoff was among the missing. His new hands were an able seaman named Joe Robinett and a tall youngster known as George Montgomery. In such brief drills as they had staged, the three had proved capable enough. The pointing of the nine-pounder and the hits it scored would be up to his own skill.

An hour passed while the sloop-of-war sped swiftly westward. They could see the strange sail plainly now, and make out that she was a full-rigged ship of about their own size. She had come about now, and was evidently trying to run away. That wasn't easy when the pursuer was the *Saratoga*.

Steadily they overhauled the fleeing ship, and before another hour went by they had her within long gun range. Young ordered a warning shot from the four-pounder in the bows. It was well aimed and they could see the splash as it fell a dozen yards from the vessel's side. An answering shot from a stern gun flew wide and skipped over the sea to starboard of the *Saratoga*. The enemy ship appeared to have no notion of heaving to. They could count the gun ports in her side and she looked well armed.

At last, when the sloop-of-war was almost within hailing distance, the ship suddenly swerved to port. In another moment her broadside would come to bear. John Young had been waiting for something of the kind. Like lightning he had the helm put hard over, and his own starboard battery faced the enemy craft.

Gid was ready. At the order to fire, his gun bellowed in unison with the others. And at the same instant he saw smoke clouds blossoming from the side of the other ship. While his men were reloading he looked aloft at the torn rigging and tattered holes in the main topsail. Then the smoke began to clear and a great cheer went up from the *Saratoga*. As the acrid cloud rolled away they could see yawning gaps in the enemy's bulwarks. There was carnage on her deck, too. One gun was tilted skyward and her crew was running about in confusion. The British flag at her peak jerked once or twice and came fluttering down.

There was no delay in getting the longboat over. Joseph Bailey, one of the new master's mates, was sent to take possession of the captured vessel with a prize crew of twenty hands. And Gid went with them to bring the prisoners back.

He was amazed at the havoc their broadside had wrought when he reached the deck. Blood was running in the scuppers and half a dozen sailors lay wounded.

Three of the eight six-pounders in the port battery had
been put out of commission.

The ship was the *Resolution*, privateer out of New
York. Her captain, John Laughton, had sighted sails to
starboard and expected an easy opportunity to cut out at
least one of the southbound merchantmen.

There were more than fifty men in the privateer's crew.
Gid got the wounded into the boat first, along with the
captain and mates, and filled it up with as many seamen as
he could carry. Then he returned for the rest.

As he clambered up the side he heard a heavy pounding
somewhere deep in the vessel's hull.

"What's that racket?" Bailey asked the ship's bosun.
"Have you got prisoners in the hold?"

The man nodded sheepishly. "I guess the skipper didn't
tell you," he said. "We took about a dozen Yankees off a
little brig out o' Jersey a few weeks ago."

"Well, get that hatch cover off and bring 'em topside,"
the master's mate ordered angrily. "Let's have a look at
'em."

The American seamen who crawled out, blinking in
the afternoon sunlight, were a sorry-looking lot, ragged
and thin. Gid paid little attention to them, for he was busy
herding prisoners into the longboat. Then he heard a voice
behind him and spun on his heel.

The man who had spoken was broad-shouldered and
burly, with a stubble of brown beard covering his face, but
Gid recognized him at once.

"Aaron!" he yelled. "How'd you get in this pickle?"

The big bayman grinned and thrust out his hand. "Hiya,

Gid?" he returned. "Just plumb stupid, I guess. Thought I could have a little fun on my leave an' wound up in this dirty tub. They've got me posted for desertin', I suppose."

Gid stopped smiling. "Yes," he said. "You're in real trouble, boy."

There were ten men besides Aaron in the captive crew. Two of them were sick with scurvy and had to be lowered over the side into the boat. When the last of his passengers was in and Gid was ready to shove off, he spoke to Bailey on deck.

"Any word for the captain, sir?" he asked. "He'll be worrying about leaks in the hull, after what happened to our last prizes."

"We've checked the wells and she's not taking any water. Tell him we'll make out fine."

Back aboard the sloop-of-war, Gid went aft at once. He approached John Young where he stood on the quarter-deck.

"Reporting all prisoners aboard, sir," the boy said. "But there's something else, sir. They had eleven Americans in the hold, and one of 'em's Aaron Mathis."

The captain's eyebrows went up and he whistled silently, rubbing his chin. Then he turned and went down the companionway.

"Tell Mr. Pyne to put Mathis under guard and send him aft," he shot over his shoulder. "I'll talk to him."

Unhappily, Gid passed the order on to the first lieutenant. And a moment later he saw his friend, flanked by two marines, marching toward the stern. Meanwhile there was a bustle of activity aboard both ships.

"Set your course nor'east by east," Pyne yelled across to Bailey. "We'll stay together as far as the Capes and start you upriver with the prize."

The winter dusk was closing in as the two vessels got under way. Gid was on deck during the first dog-watch, and Allison assigned him to the wheel. He was becoming a fair helmsman now. But with the wind from the north they had to run close-hauled to hold their course, and that required sharp steering.

He was too preoccupied with his job to see Aaron leave the cabin. A few minutes later, however, Captain Young came up to pace the quarter-deck behind him. Nervous, the boy tightened his grip, easing the constant kick of the wheel. Every few seconds he looked aloft to see how the sails were drawing. The rest of the time he had to keep his eyes riveted on the compass.

He heard the steady rhythm of the captain's footsteps change. Then Young was standing at his elbow.

"Good," the older man grunted. "She'll point up a bit more, though. Give her a shade of starboard helm. That's better."

After a moment he went on talking. "About your friend Mathis," he said. "I think we'll forget the whole thing. The new men in the crew won't know the difference, and the old hands would resent it if we sent him to jail. But the main thing is, he's too good a man to lose. He was honest with me—knew he'd done a foolish thing and offered no excuses. I'm going to cross out the desertion entry and put his name back on the rolls."

Gid swallowed hard. "Thanks, sir," he mumbled. "I don't think you'll be sorry."

*   *   *

If he had not had so many prisoners aboard, Captain Young would probably have returned at once to the convoy. As it was, he believed the *Confederacy* had followed them out of the Delaware and must have overtaken the merchant fleet before now. So he steered for the Capes, escorting the newly captured prize.

Before midnight the wind swung northeasterly and the ships were forced to tack, beating their way slowly back to the coast.

Christmas Eve found them still a good many leagues offshore. The sea was rough, the wind cold and contrary, and nobody aboard had much heart for celebrating the ancient festival. Gid wore his knitted cap that bitter evening, grateful to Peggy Lane for knitting real warmth into it. When they came off watch at midnight, the midshipmen sang a carol or two, led by Jack Livingston's clear tenor voice. Then they turned in.

Gid lay thinking of other Christmases, down by the Mullica, and felt a pang of homesickness.

It wasn't until New Year's Day, 1781, that the *Saratoga* dropped her anchor off Lewes. The boat that went ashore carried letters and brought back the news. The *Confederacy*, as Young had expected, had cleared Cape Henlopen on December twenty-first, the day after they had left. It

153

was presumed that she was now in company with the convoy and well down into the West Indies. However, the *Saratoga's* orders were to sail to the same destination, so they wasted no time in port.

The prisoners were transferred to the *Resolution* and her prize crew took her up the Delaware. That same day, January first, the sloop-of-war headed for sea.

All but two of the men from the *Absecon* had signed on for naval service in the *Saratoga,* so that she now had a full compliment of men, plenty of supplies and enough powder and shot for as many engagements as she was likely to have to fight. The veteran hands imparted much of their skill and spirit to the newer men, and constant drill kept them all on their toes. The ship was a dangerous opponent for any vessel up to nearly double her size and gun power.

In two days of fair winds they made their easting, then swung southward. Once they were past Cape Hatteras they could feel the difference in the air. Even the northerly breeze lost its sting in those latitudes. They bowled on at an easy gait, keeping a sharp lookout for possible enemy sails.

On January fifth they were right in the edge of the Gulf Stream. To starboard the sea was still gray and wintry. To port it showed the deep blue tinge of the tropics. Everyone on deck who was not busy put a handline over the side and fished. The bait varied from salt pork to bits of bright cloth. At first there were few bites. Then one of the seamen hauled in a bonito and let his mates cut strips of it to put on the hooks. That made a real difference. Almost immediately they began to catch fish and there were hundreds flopping on the deck when Allison called a halt to the fun.

Prince Gilbert, the Negro cook, rubbed his huge hands and beamed. For two days the crew ate chowder and fried fish instead of salt-horse.

As they held their course southward the temperature seemed to rise every day. Pea jackets and sea boots were discarded. The men worked in their shirts, and many of them went barefoot. With some regret Gid put his knitted cap into his sea chest, to wait for a time when he might need it again.

He was taking lessons in navigation from Lieutenant Pyne now. Daily, at noon, they used the sextant and plotted the ship's position.

"Cap'n Young told me to give you some instruction," said the South Carolinian. "That's a good sign. Looks as if he meant to let you command a prize some time soon."

Gid agreed that he was probably right. In any case, he wanted to know how to navigate if the occasion should ever arise. He studied the stars as well as the sun, and when the second lieutenant tested his knowledge he passed with a good score.

The balmy days continued and the wind grew lighter as they moved down the broad blue path of the Gulf Stream. The log showed fewer knots each day. Perhaps they were too far to the west to find British sail. At any rate, Young gave orders for the course to be changed, and they cruised southwest. At that time Gid's calculations showed that they were some hundred leagues off the coast of the colony of Georgia.

Though no one aboard the *Saratoga* knew it, the ship was advancing toward the greatest battle of her career.

Some time in the first week of January a large letter-of-marque ship called the *Tonyn* had sailed out of St. Augustine, the capital of His Majesty's loyal province of East Florida. She was a good-sized vessel and well found. Armed with twenty long nine-pounders and manned by a crew of more than a hundred men, she was considered a fair match for anything the Americans had to offer, up to the rating of a frigate. And it is quite probable that her gallant skipper, Captain John Wade, would have given battle to a Yankee frigate if necessary.

The *Tonyn* carried a valuable cargo. In her hold were barrels of turpentine and indigo, barrel staves and bales of hides and deerskins. She was bound for Liverpool, in England.

The morning of January ninth was bright and the sun shone warm. The crew of the *Saratoga* had eaten breakfast and set topgallantsails and skysails to make up for the lightness of the wind. She was standing southwestward with all her canvas drawing.

Gid was in the main top, a few feet higher than Nat Penfield, who had the lookout at the fore crosstrees. They had seen no sail for days on end and possibly young Penfield had grown careless. In any case it was the South Jersey lad who sighted the white speck first.

"Deck, ho!" he yelled. "There's a sail dead ahead!"

He saw Nat Penfield snap out of his trance and stare forward. "That's right!" the other midshipman called. "I've got her now—not more than half a point to starboard!"

WITH WELL-ORDERED SPEED the *Saratoga* cleared for action. All movable gear was stripped from the deck. Shot was piled handy to the cannon. Fire tubs were filled with water and sand. And the powder monkeys raced forward and aft with bags of good French gunpowder for the carriage guns.

There was no need to change course. The other ship was headed straight for them. They could see her lofty headsails now, and the Union Jack flying proudly from her main top. In answer, John Young ran up his own Stars and Stripes.

In the gun-deck, Gid was busy loading his nine-pounder. The same exultant spirit that could be seen in the actions of the rest of the crew filled his little squad. Tom Pilkinton grinned at him as he hauled at the tackle, and the muscles stood out like ropes on his broad back.

The two ships drew steadily closer, neither one giving an inch. At a distance of five or six hundred yards, Captain Young ordered the helm hard over to port. Gracefully the *Saratoga* came about, running on a parallel course with her adversary and almost abeam. That was when they saw the ten gun ports in the *Tonyn's* side, and the menacing black muzzles of her battery.

The word was passed quietly: "Ready a starboard broadside." Then Young picked up his speaking trumpet.

"Strike your flag!" he bellowed. "This is the Continental sloop-of-war *Saratoga,* John Young commanding. What ship is that?"

The name of the American ship was one to strike terror into the heart of a merchant skipper. Her many victories had been recounted in the Tory papers of New York and Charleston. But Captain Wade was not easily daunted.

They heard his calm reply coming across the water. "This is the *Tonyn,* letter-of-marque, John R. Wade commanding. St. Augustine to Liverpool. Strike your own flag!"

He must have given the command to fire in the same breath, for the long nines roared and the balls screamed through the rigging over Gid's head. The boy was watching for Allison's signal. When the lieutenant brought his arm down, Gid laid the slow-match to the priming. He had sighted carefully, aiming a little above the *Tonyn's* waterline, and Allison timed the broadside so that all the starboard guns could fire just as the rolling ship reached an even keel.

The smoke lay too thick between the two vessels for anyone to see what effect their fire had had. But they were too busy reloading to look. The starboard guns were hauled back in unison. Into their barrels plunged the steaming swabs. Then the powder bags and the round shot were rammed home and they were run out again. The long hours of drill counted then. Neither ship had veered and Gid could see the masts of the enemy only fifty yards away through the drifting smoke.

"Fire as you bear!" Lieutenant Allison bellowed. And Gid laid the gun and applied the match within seconds after the command.

The battle continued in full fury for half an hour, with the starboard battery bearing the brunt of the fighting. Many of the men from the port side came over to help serve the hot and smoking guns.

Gid had no idea how many times he fired, but there was no letup, no respite for tired arms and aching lungs. Men began to drop beside their cannon out of sheer exhaustion. They were dragged back out of the way, and others sprang to take their places.

Once a powder bag caught fire from the smoldering wood of Gid's gun carriage. Without a second's hesitation young Montgomery seized it and heaved it over the side where it burst into a roar of flames before it fell hissing into the water.

After what seemed like an eternity the order came to hold their fire. Half deafened, Gid didn't hear the words. He would have dropped his match to the touch-hole again if a fellow gunner hadn't held his arm. Dazed and gasping for breath, the boy staggered back and looked about him with smarting, red-rimmed eyes.

Out of the thinning smoke the side of the *Tonyn*
loomed, so close it startled him. The British flag had come
down from the peak and the deck of the ship was a
shambles. Her long nine-pounders lay every which way,
not a single gun in the port battery still able to fire. A
young officer, his head bandaged and blood running down
his face, stood dejectedly by the mainmast foot. There
were wounded men lying around him but only a bare
handful of the crew were still able to stand.

Aboard the *Saratoga* the sails were torn to ribbons and
half the cordage had been cut. The weary men squatted
about the deck, grinning through smoke-blackened lips.
But to Gid's amazement not one of them appeared to have
suffered more than a scratch or two.

The two ships were pulled together with grappling
hooks, and a boarding party under Lieutenant Pyne scrambled over the shattered bulwarks. When they came back
they told a grim story. In one of the first volleys of the
battle a flying splinter had struck Captain Wade, wounding
him so badly that he had to be carried below. The first
lieutenant who took his place was knocked out fifteen minutes later. The cockpit, by then, was filled with wounded
and dying men, but the youthful second lieutenant fought
on bravely. At last, with all his guns out of action and half
his crew disabled, he saw the *Saratoga* closing in to board
him. And so he struck his colors.

Dr. Brown was rushed to the other ship, for her surgeon
had far more than he could do. The *Tonyn's* casualty list
showed seven men killed and more than fifty wounded.
Among them were nearly all her officers.

It took the rest of that day to straighten up the sloop-of-war, repair the rigging and bend on new canvas from the sail lockers. Then another day passed before the British ship could be made seaworthy. Captain Wade and his wounded lieutenants were brought aboard the *Saratoga*, where Surgeon Brown could give them better care. The men of the crew were made as comfortable as possible in their own cockpit. And such prisoners as were uninjured went into the hold of the sloop-of-war.

Damages to the prize were many, but by luck or good shooting she had no holes below the waterline. Young put a good-sized crew aboard her, and on the eleventh of January they headed southward together. It was the Yankee captain's idea that the *Tonyn's* cargo would fetch a higher price in the West Indies than in Philadelphia. Also, he felt she would be safer from winter storms or enemy cruisers if she stayed in southern waters. So he decided to take her with him into Cap François.

That was an easy voyage. Such breezes as they had were mostly southerly, so the ships continued to beat to windward. The air was as soft as a June zephyr. Bareheaded and coatless, Gid stood in the bows by the hour when he was off duty, drinking in the scent of tropic islands off there beyond the sea's rim. At night the men left their stuffy quarters below decks and slept under the stars.

Captain Young thought his crew deserved a little relaxation following their last engagement. However, he saw to it that they didn't grow too lazy. After the first three days he had them holystoning the deck and drilling at the guns again.

None of the four midshipmen had ever visited the tropics before, and they looked forward eagerly to making port in Haiti. Often they talked about it among themselves.

"If old Sam Clarkson was only here he could tell us," said Jack Livingston. "Sam made a voyage to Martinique in 'seventy-nine aboard the *Confederacy*. I remember he had a lot of tales about the fruit—bananas and mangoes and oranges—and the parrots in the palm trees.

"And the French Creole belles," Barent Sebring put in.

"I don't suppose you mere youths are interested in that sort o' thing, but wait till I get ashore!"

Nat Penfield was more practical. "I hope we get a whopping price out o' the *Tonyn*," he said. "It'll be nice to go home with a pocketful o' hard money—half joes or whatever they use for coin down there."

"And don't forget," Gid reminded them, "we're going to help win the war by bringing back those supplies for General Washington's troops that Monsieur Carabasse is supposed to have ready for us."

So they dreamed and planned and wished for a fair wind, to bring them sooner to the islands.

A full week after the capture of the *Tonyn*, Gid shot the sun at noon and worked out their position. His reckoning, checked by Lieutenant Blaney Allison, showed their lattitude as 24° North and their longitude 72° 30′ West. On the chart that put them about fifty leagues eastward of the Bahamas. He would remember those bearings for a long time to come.

Hardly had he put away the sextant when the lookout reported a sail on the port quarter. "She looks to be brig-rigged," he called down, "an' headed nor'east."

"Port your helm," Captain Young shouted. "Clear the decks for action!"

The *Saratoga* came about smartly on a course that would intercept the brig's, and the *Tonyn* hove to, waiting to see what happened. The wind had freshened a little. With all sails set, the fastest ship in the American Navy raced down on her quarry.

Soon they could see the brig's hull. She wasn't very big, and her bulwarks were pierced for only three guns on a side. As soon as they came within range a four-pound shot was laid across her bows and they saw her flag flutter down as she came up into the wind.

"Midshipman Jones," John Young ordered, "take twenty men in the longboat and board her. Arm your crew with cutlasses and don't stand for any trouble."

Thrilled at the chance, Gid slipped into his uniform coat and stuck a pistol in his belt while the boat was being lowered. The *Saratoga* lay only forty yards from the brig, and a dozen strokes of the oars carried the longboat to her side.

"Drop a ladder, there," the boy yelled from the sternsheets.

The Jacob's ladder was lowered at once and he grasped the rungs, scrambling quickly to the deck.

A dozen sailors stood about, watching him with sullen eyes.

"Who's in command here?" he snapped, and a portly, gray-haired man in a blue coat stepped forward.

"Captain Archibald Gregg of the brig *Douglass*," he replied. "Madeira to Charleston. And what ship is yours, young sir, if I may ask?"

The heavy irony in his tone nettled Gid. "The Continental sloop-of-war *Saratoga*," he replied. "Midshipman Gideon Jones, at your service, sir. My orders are to accept your surrender or take you by force."

By this time he had a score of Yankee cutlasses at his

back, and the *Saratoga's* gun muzzles loomed ominously close. The British captain announced in some haste that he wanted no bloodshed. They would surrender, of course.

"Line the prisoners up," Gid ordered. "Search them for arms and see if there are any more below."

While this was being done he marched Captain Gregg to his cabin and demanded the brig's manifest and other papers. A glance through them told the boy that this was no ordinary prize. He returned with the captain to the deck, left enough men aboard to handle the sails, and was rowed back to the sloop-of-war with his prisoners.

John Young was waiting on the quarter-deck. He greeted the British skipper courteously, then took the manifest which Gid had brought him. As he scanned it, his face lit up. Half to himself he read the items:

"Twenty pipes, twenty hogsheads of the finest old Madeira wine; thirty pipes, ten hogsheads, twenty quarter casks of London market ditto; seventy pipes, ten hogsheads, twenty quarter casks of New York market ditto; seventy-five pipes, one hundred hogsheads, one hundred quarter casks of best cargo ditto; nineteen boxes of Poland starch."

Madeira wine was highly regarded in Philadelphia, and for the past few years the British blockade had made the supply short. Young thought of the brisk bidding such a cargo would command at home and smiled.

He called Lieutenant Allison to show Captain Gregg to his quarters, then beckoned Gid inside his cabin and closed the door.

"Gideon," he said familiarly, laying a hand on the boy's shoulder, "how would you like to take this prize to Philadelphia?"

Gid flushed with pleasure and pride. "I'd like to try it, sir," he answered.

"It won't be easy," Young told him. "You'll have to lay a course well away from the coast, then trust to luck and the weather when you make your run for the Delaware. By now I expect those waters are swarming with frigates and privateers. But I'd rather risk it, in this case, than take the brig to Haiti. Her cargo'll bring double or triple the price if we can get her to Philadelphia."

The boy nodded respectfully. "Yes, sir," he said.

"They tell me you've picked up a fair bit of navigation," the captain went on. "I can spare a good crew, though I don't expect you to do any fighting. What sort of armament does she carry?"

"Only eight guns that I saw," Gid replied. "All six-pounders. Two of 'em are swivels, mounted bow and stern. I didn't have a chance to look into the magazine or the shot locker."

Young grinned. "Well," he said, "let's hope you don't have to fire those guns. The brig looks smart enough and her canvas is new. A fair turn of speed, I'd judge. Good luck to you, lad, and you can move your dunnage over to the captain's cabin at once. Who'd be your choice for a mate?"

Gid had already thought of that. "If I could have him, sir, I'd like Aaron Mathis. He's a better sailor than I, and the men will take orders from him."

Young stroked his chin and nodded. "That's settled, then," he said. "I'll let him help me pick a crew."

Gid was fairly treading on air as he sped to the midshipmen's berth to gather his belongings. He blurted out the story of his luck to Jack Livingston, who heard the news with genuine pleasure.

"I won't say I'm not jealous." The governor's son grinned. "But it's a fine chance for you and you deserve it. I'll content myself with basking in the tropics, and see you back home when the cruise is over."

On deck Gid found his prize crew drawn up under Aaron's stern eye. There were twenty men in the group—enough to handle the brig in any weather. Six of them were Jersey baymen off the *Absecon,* and the rest were all seasoned hands who had been in the sloop-of-war from the beginning. Aaron had also signed the cook from the *Douglass*—a small, grizzled Negro who had volunteered for the post.

Gid asked him his name and whether he was a slave. The answer came in a strange British dialect.

"My name called Hercules," he said proudly. "I belong no mahster. I am me own mahn."

Captain Young handed Gid a hastily written letter to Francis Lewis and a note to Mistress Young. Then the prize crew got into the longboat and rowed over to the brig. The men who had been left to guard her took the boat back, and both vessels prepared to make sail.

Standing on his own quarter-deck, Gid supervised the operation, then turned to wave good-bye. The *Saratoga* was already heeled far over to starboard, skimming the sea like a great white gull. She was so beautiful, the sight of her leaving brought a lump in his throat. With a strange premonition, he wondered at that moment if he would ever see her again.

BEFORE THE SLOOP-OF-WAR had vanished over the horizon, the young prize captain found plenty to occupy him. First he made an inspection of the ship with Aaron accompanying him. She seemed to be well found in provisions and the food in the lockers was of better quality than they had known in the *Saratoga*. Hercules was already busy in the small, neat galley. They sniffed at the soup he had on the stove and it smelled good.

There was a fair amount of powder in the magazine, as well as eighty or ninety rounds of shot. An arms locker contained a dozen muskets, and ammunition to use in them.

They tested the wells and found the hull was taking no water. As soon as the sails were set and drawing properly, Aaron assigned watches. The course he gave the helmsman was due north. Gid got out the charts and saw that a bearing had been taken at noon of that day, January 16th. The brig's log gave him some facts of interest. She appeared to have made a good voyage across the Atlantic, in spite of a week when she lay becalmed in the doldrums.

With a fair wind astern or abeam she had logged better than two hundred miles on some of her better days.

The boy was busy charting a course that would take them about midway between Bermuda and Cape Fear when his mate knocked at the door.

"Skipper," he said, as Gid looked up, "I've found one thing I don't like. It's the water in the butts. There ain't too much of it, an' what there is has got green scum floatin' in it."

Gid frowned. "That's bad, when we've got two or three weeks more ahead of us," he said. "Let's see when they filled their casks." The log showed no mention of watering when the vessel was taking cargo at Funchal, in the Madeiras.

"No wonder it's stale," said Aaron. "Must ha' been carried all the way from England. Well, maybe we can make it do for tea an' soup. One good thing—I found a couple o' kegs o' lime juice. That'll keep us from gettin' scurvy."

A westerly breeze gave them easy sailing for the next two days. Gid kept a sharp lookout aloft day and night. And Aaron gave the men some practice at the guns, particularly the brass swivel mounted on the poop.

"Could be we'll get chased," he told Gid. "An' I'd like to be sure we land at least one shot before we're caught."

Between these activities the men had some time to fish and they made the most of it. One of them pulled in a horse-mackerel that weighed close to a hundred pounds. Sliced into steaks and fried in the galley it gave them a tremendous supper that night.

The first complaints about the water came from the

Mullica River men. They weren't used to long voyages and knew little about the rigors of life in a man-of-war. The old hands laughed at them but the grumbling continued, out of the officers' hearing.

Then one night Aaron found a cargo hatch open. Letting himself down into the hold he came upon two of the crew about to tap a cask of wine. He drove them on deck with a belaying pin, mustered all hands and laid down the law.

"Next man I catch doin' that'll get a dozen lashes an' be put in irons," he announced grimly.

But in the privacy of the after cabin he let Gid know that he was worried. "Those were two o' my boys," he said. "I don't like to have trouble with 'em, but trouble there'll be, sure as shootin', unless we get some fresh water."

"I don't doubt that," Gid agreed. "But there's no land nearer than a hundred leagues, and that's under the Crown. What's more, if we did put in at one o' those little coral islands the chances are 'twould be dry. The folks that live on 'em don't dig wells. They catch rain water in cisterns. I reckon about all we can do is pray for rain ourselves."

The next morning dawned clear and cloudless and the wind held fair abeam. Gid waited till noon and shot the sun. The position he got bore out his dead reckoning. They had made just under a hundred and eighty sea miles in the past twenty-four hours. He was marking the new position on the chart when he heard a hail from the masthead.

"There's some sort o' craft dead ahead," the lookout called. "No sails—she's driftin' under bare poles."

Gid took a glass from the rack and climbed the companion steps. "Helm over a bit," he told the steersman. "I
want to get a look at whatever it is ahead."

Through the telescope he saw a black hull with a foremast, the stump of a mainmast, and a few gray shreds of
canvas blowing from the spars. On the new course the
Douglass would draw alongside her in another ten minutes.

"Want me to beat to quarters?" Aaron asked.

"No need," said Gid. "She's been abandoned. Take a
look for yourself."

The mate stared through the glass for a full minute.
"You're right," he said. "Not a man in sight, and nobody
at the helm, the way she's yawin'. Might as well go on an'
forget her."

"No," Gid told him. "We're going to board her. Ought
to know what happened, in case she's American. Get the
gig ready to launch an' see what you can find."

They swept down abreast of the drifting hulk and hove
to. Aaron and four seamen rowed across to the vessel and
scaled the side while Gid and the rest of the crew watched.
The little boarding party scattered to explore the cabin
and fo'c's'le.

They were within easy hailing distance and after two or
three minutes there came an excited shout. "Water!" cried
one of the searchers. "She's got plenty o' fresh water in
the butts!"

Gid ordered a larger boat over the side at once. "Bring
back as many casks as you can handle," he told the men at
the oars.

They made two trips, transporting a dozen big water barrels to the brig. Then Aaron's party returned and the boats were hoisted in.

"What did you make of her?" Gid asked his mate when they had left the derelict behind.

Aaron shook his head. "It's hard to say. No papers in the cabin an' no sign of a battle. The letters on her transom are only half there, but they might be part of a name like *Andrew* or *Andrea*. I'd guess she was a brig, out o' Bermuda maybe, or Jamaica. All her boats are gone, so I reckon she was wrecked in a storm an' her crew left her."

"Bad luck for them," Gid grinned. "But good for us. Anyhow it's settled our water problem for the rest o' the voyage!"

The prize crew had opportunity to test the *Douglass* in various kinds of wind and weather during the next ten days. She proved better before the wind than tacking, but at least they found her seaworthy. The twentieth of January was a dark, squally day and toward evening it came on to blow with considerable fury from the northeast. She rode out the brief storm under double-reefed topsails. Though she was blown off to leeward some sixty miles in the course of the night, they had her beating gallantly back into a stiff breeze by noon of the next day.

After that the winds were uncertain. Gid took sights whenever he was able and plotted the course with care. But for a full week the log showed an average gain of less than a hundred miles a day.

On the twenty-ninth they had reached the latitude of Charleston, in South Carolina, and according to the young commander's reckoning were still well off the coast. Not far enough, however, as they learned that day.

The lookout may have grown careless from staring so long at an empty ocean. At any rate it was Aaron, standing near the wheel, who first noticed the sail to port.

"You, up there!" he yelled angrily. "Why don't you hail when you see a ship? What d' you make of her?"

There was some hesitation aloft, and the mate started up the ratlines himself. Then at last the word came down.

"She's a brig!" the man announced breathlessly. " 'Bout our size—maybe four miles off an' headed this way."

Any ship encountered in those British waters was more likely to be hostile than friendly. Aaron cracked on more sail and Gid had the helm put over to starboard. They started a long reach to the east, with the northerly wind abeam. It was then about two o'clock in the afternoon.

Running on parallel courses the two brigs seemed for a while to hold the same relative positions. Then, watching their pursuer with the glass, Gid realized she must be gaining little by little. He could make out her gun ports now, and the British Jack flying at her peak. He handed the telescope to Aaron.

"How many guns?" he asked.

The other lad studied the other brig's side. "Five in the starboard battery—maybe six. An' they're likely to be nine-pounders. What do you aim to do? Put up a fight?"

"Not if I can get out of it. Can't you find some way to give us a little more speed?"

Aaron looked aloft gloomily. "She's carryin' every stitch now. Guess I'd better load that stern gun, at least."

Gid nodded. "Go ahead," he said.

They had not been able to find an American flag in the lockers of the *Douglass* and so she was sailing without displaying any colors at all. The chase went on and on. It was nearing sunset before the pursuing brig came within long cannon range.

Watching from his post on the afterdeck, Gid saw a puff of smoke blossom from the enemy's bow. Then, at almost the same instant that he heard the *boom* of the gun, a ball came skipping over the water and sank short of the stern.

Aaron had the swivel gun loaded and was raising the muzzle to what looked like the proper elevation for a long shot.

"All right," Gid told him. "Did you put in a good heavy powder charge? See what you can do."

The report shook the deck as he fired. With the wind abeam the smoke was quickly carried away, and they saw a white splash right under the vessel's forefoot.

"Hit her, by golly!" Aaron cried exultantly. But if he was right, the shot appeared to have no effect on the enemy's speed. Little by little she continued to gain, while the gun crew swabbed out the six-pounder and reloaded.

Once more the other brig let go with its bow gun. This time the screaming roundshot flew a few feet over Gid's head and ripped a hole through the spanker. The boy set his jaw grimly. Now that they had the range the next one might do real damage. He ran forward to the waiting gunners in the waist.

"Are all your guns loaded?" he asked. "I want a starboard broadside when I give the word. We'll come about and cross her bows. Aim right at the foremast and make every shot count. We may never get another chance."

With that he vaulted back to the raised quarter-deck and was at Aaron's side when he fired the swivel again. There was no doubt about it this time. They could see the dark splinters fly where the shot crashed into the Britisher's bow just below the fore-chains.

"Nice shooting, Aaron!" Gid cried. "Now you're in charge o' the ship. Wait about a minute and put her hard over to starboard, before they know what we're doing. I'd like to cut right across her bows and rake her with the starboard guns."

The mate nodded, grinned and took the wheel. "Tell those fellers in the port battery to leave their guns," he instructed the man he replaced. "Get 'em at the braces, ready to pull fast when we come about."

Gid meanwhile was running from one starboard gun to another, checking the priming, lifting or lowering each barrel to the elevation he wanted. He turned and signaled to Aaron, and as the helm went over the brig spun on her heel. She came into the wind with a rush, hung there for a few seconds with sails slatting, then filled away on the opposite tack as the yards were trimmed.

The young skipper waited tensely, sighting along the barrel of the first gun. When the bow of the oncoming brig was just coming into line, he yelled "Fire!" and jumped back to watch.

The first and second cannon fired together. The third, delayed a bare two seconds, was caught by the roll of the

ship and its shot went high. Every man aboard held his breath, waiting for the smoke to clear. Then a wild, ragged cheer went up. The foremast of the brig, shattered right at the crosstrees, toppled and fell to leeward in a frightful tangle of cordage and canvas.

"Take her about again!" Gid shouted to Aaron. "We've got to stay for'ard of 'em or they'll bring a broadside to bear!"

Once more the young mate swung the wheel and the brig's crew executed the maneuver beautifully. The *Douglass* was well out of range before the enemy ship fell off enough to train her broadside guns.

"She's disabled!" called Aaron. "How about rakin' her again an' then tryin' to board her?"

For a moment Gid was tempted. Then he shook his head. "I reckon she's a privateer," he said. "Probably seventy or eighty men in her, an' twice our weight in metal. It'll be coming on dark pretty quick, an' before they're able to clear away that foremast wreckage we can leave her a long way behind."

They scudded off to the northward in the gathering dusk, while the British brig wallowed helplessly astern.

Aaron sent the starboard watch below for supper, then came back to Gid's side. "You decided right," he said. "Guess I got carried away, after those shots landed. Boy, that was shootin'! Made me proud to serve under you."

17

THEY RAN INTO FOG and storms off Cape Hatteras. It was normal weather for those latitudes—the time of winter gales. It was fortunate that Gid's course had allowed plenty of sea room, for the wind blew gustily out of the east. And though they tried to beat northward there was a constant drift toward the Carolina coast.

Neither Gid nor Aaron undressed for more than seventy hours. They were on deck night and day, and such sleep as they got was only in brief snatches. The brig handled well, and she was staunchly built. For the better part of a week she took the pounding of heavy seas without springing any serious leaks.

Twice they saw distant sails, but fog or darkness shut down in time to protect them from possible pursuit. Gid's whole thought now was centered on getting his prize into the Delaware. He wanted no more adventures until the brig and her cargo were safely delivered.

By such dead reckoning as he had been able to keep, they were some forty leagues east of Cape Henlopen on the eleventh of February. That morning the wind shifted, the skies began to clear, and at noon he was able to take a sight on the sun. Then he worked out his calculations and stared frowning at the chart. A recheck showed the figures were right. In haste he jumped up from the table and ran to the companionway. They were much nearer the coast than he had thought.

"Aaron!" he yelled. "Send another lookout aloft! We'll raise the Delaware Capes by evening if I'm not wrong in my figuring. An' this close to the bay we're likely to run into trouble."

They hoisted all the sail the brig would carry and scudded along on a southerly wind with sharp-eyed men in the fore and main tops. At five o'clock they sighted Cape Henlopen dead ahead against the reddening sky of sunset. And ten minutes later Gid's fears were justified. They sighted a sail to the northward.

As soon as the lookout told the deck, Gid took the glass and raced up the ratlines to the main crosstrees. The headland, he judged, was roughly five miles to leeward—half an hour's sailing if the wind held. The ship, whose royals and topgallantsails were now clearly visible, lay about the same distance off their starboard beam. From her size and rig he knew she was a British man-of-war and certainly no smaller than a frigate.

She must have sighted the *Douglass* by now, for he saw her change her course. Where she had been on a westward tack she suddenly came about and headed southeasterly. She might have a mile or two more distance to cover than the brig, but her new course was meant to intercept theirs.

Gid and his mate held a hurried council of war. If they had been in the *Saratoga* they might have stood a chance with a frigate, either fighting or running. As it was, they both agreed that a stern chase would be fatal. All they could do was keep on as they were. Reaching, on a beam wind, they had a slight advantage, for the other ship would be forced to beat to windward.

"Anything you can do to get more speed out of her?" the young prize captain asked.

Aaron looked aloft and shook his head. "She's got every stitch drawin' now," he said. "Only thing we could do is heave the carriage guns over. That'd lighten her a bit, but there's no tellin' if she'd sail faster."

"No," Gid decided. "I won't do it—not yet anyhow. They're good guns an' they might help us before we're through."

Ten minutes passed, then twenty, and the land loomed nearer on the port bow. Meanwhile the other vessel was bowling along a scant two miles away. She was no longer right abeam but a little toward the starboard quarter. In the fading light they could see her hull now and count the three white tiers of gun ports in her dark side. A seventy-four gun ship-of-the-line!

Gid drew a shaky breath. If she ever came within range, she could blow the little *Douglass* clean out of water. But could she get that close? He shut his eyes and prayed devoutly that their favoring wind would hold.

"We're past the cape!" Aaron cried. "There's the lighthouse at Lewes. She'll never catch us now!"

And sure enough, as darkness settled over the sea they

saw the big Britisher come into the wind and swing away on the opposite tack. She had no wish to tangle with a possible American squadron inside the bay.

Gid anchored at the Delaware port overnight and picked up a pilot in the morning. The southerly wind that still blew gave them a good start up the bay. By nightfall they reached Chester, where the first pilot was dropped and another, familiar with the upper river, came aboard next morning.

The sky was overcast and there were spits of snow in the wind when they weighed anchor. Even with a helping tide the trip was slow and hazardous. It was close to three in the afternoon when they finally threaded the channel through the chevaux-de-frise and moored the brig off the Philadelphia docks.

Gid gave strict orders that all must stay aboard until he learned what disposition would be made of the prize. Two men rowed him and the pilot ashore and he hurried up the hill to Commissioner Francis Lewis's office on Front Street. He was afraid the chairman of the Admiralty Board might have left for the day, and in fact he saw his carriage just pulling away from the door. Running after it, he hailed Mr. Lewis through the window of the coach.

The driver stopped the horses. "What's this?" fumed the florid gentleman inside. He must have taken Gid for a beggar of some sort until he caught sight of the rumpled uniform.

"Why, bless my soul!" he exclaimed then. "It's Mr. Smith—no, Mr. Jones, out o' John Young's sloop-o'-war!

Step in here, my boy. It's too cold to stand about in the street."

Gid got into the carriage and gave the commissioner a brief account of the capture of the *Douglass*. "She's lying just off High Street," he finished. "And here's her manifest, sir."

Lewis took the proffered paper and scanned it rapidly. As he read, his eyes fairly popped out.

"Egad, Mr. Jones!" he said at last. "This is the richest prize taken in a year! And the city's famished for good Madeira. We'll get top prices and a quick sale, I warrant, as soon as the brig's been condemned."

"That's fine, sir," the boy replied. "What should I do about the crew in the meantime? Do you expect to pay them off?"

Lewis changed color and *harrumphed* once or twice. "Er, the way finances stand at the moment, I doubt if there are enough funds for that," he answered. "When you've turned the brig over to the Admiralty marshal, I suggest you set 'em ashore on indefinite leave, subject to immediate recall, o' course, if their services are required. How soon does Captain Young expect to return?"

"I've a letter for you from the captain, sir," said Gid, and placed it in Lewis's hand. The commissioner began to read.

"Ah—'proceeding to Cap François with the prize ship *Tonyn*, captured after severe fighting'—hm—'cruise in southern waters—return about April first with military supplies now held by Monsieur Carabasse.' "

He turned to Gid. "There's your answer, young man. Today's the thirteenth and it may be two weeks before the brig is libeled against. When that time comes I'd give your men four weeks' leave—have 'em report back the last day o' March. That includes you, too, o' course. When Young gets here he'll need you in the *Saratoga.*"

Gid rode with him as far as Laurel Street, where he delivered the captain's note to Mistress Young. Then he walked back to the wharf through the gathering gloom, and was rowed out to the *Douglass.* In the cabin he told Aaron about his conversation with Mr. Lewis.

"No pay, o' course," he concluded. "The men won't like that, an' some of 'em are pretty sure to disappear. But what else can we do? We won't even have a ship a week or so from now."

Aaron shook his head. "Like you say, it's bad," he agreed. "The only thing might bring 'em back is the chance to get their prize shares. I reckon when Young comes home he'll see to it we get some money, one way or another."

Through the next nine or ten days the young captain and his mate kept the crew as busy as they could. When the weather cleared, the deck was holystoned, the superstructure painted and the bright work polished. If the appearance of the brig would have any effect on the price bid for her, they intended she should be as taut and shining as elbow grease could make her.

On the afternoon of the eleventh day Commissioner Lewis came aboard with Secretary Brown of the Board of Admiralty. They went over the vessel from stem to stern and complimented Gid and Aaron on bringing her through the stormy Atlantic in such good shape.

"I don't suppose you've had occasion to test these guns," Lewis remarked, half jokingly.

Gid reddened. "Yes, sir," he said. "We not only had to use 'em but I guess they saved our skins. I didn't mention it before, but there was a heavy-gunned privateer after us, off Charleston. We managed to put his foremast out o' commission with a broadside an' got away."

Lewis was astonished. "That must have taken good shooting and good sailing," he exclaimed. "Young'll be proud of his officers."

He went on to tell them that the marshal would take over the brig next day. "You won't need the crew any more," he said. "Let them have a month's leave. If you'd like to stay aboard until the sale takes place, I see no reason why you shouldn't. Or, if you'd rather go home at once, you're at liberty to do so."

They talked it over when Lewis and Brown had gone. Neither of the boys had much money, and living aboard the brig for a few days would save the expense of an inn. On the other hand they would have to eat ship's rations. Aaron wrinkled his nose at that idea.

"We're not obliged to stay, 'cordin' to Mr. Lewis," he said. "Me, I'd like to get back to my ma's cookin'."

Gid felt very much the same way, but the brig had been his first command. It seemed to him he had a duty to see that she was safely sold. They mustered all hands early next morning and sent them off with passes for a month's shore leave. When Aaron, too, went over the side with

his sea-bag, Gid felt very much alone and somewhat regretted his decision. But half an hour later he was glad
he had stayed.

A boat with eight or ten men came out to the *Douglass*
and a sour-faced clerk mounted the ladder. He announced
that he was taking possession in the marshal's name, and
would berth the brig at the prize wharf. Several of the
hands he brought aboard were tipsy and none of them
looked like real seamen. Somewhat stiffly Gid asked the
fellow for his credentials.

The paper he produced was genuine enough and bore
Francis Lewis's own signature. But it was a trial of the
young midshipman's temper to watch the lubberly way
they went about hoisting sail and bringing up the anchor.
Finally he bore a hand at the halyards himself. When
there was enough sail spread to give her steerage way he
took over the helm.

Luckily the tide was just at the turn and he was able to
steer the brig in alongside the wharf without cracking her
timbers. Once she was made fast and her sails furled,
the clerk and his crew departed. A watchman on the dock
seemed to be the only guard provided for the prize and
her cargo.

It was nearing noon then and Gid was hungry. He
started from his cabin to go to the galley when a wizened
brown face appeared in the companionway.

"Yes, sar," said Hercules with a grin that showed all
his teeth. "Your dinner is ready, Captain, sar."

"Wh-what are you doing aboard?" Gid asked in aston-
ishment.

"I tole you, sar," the little Negro replied. "I am me own mahn. I choose stay in de ship an' cook for you, Captain."

Gid swallowed his amusement and nodded curtly as an officer should. "Very good, Hercules," he said. "I thought you'd gone ashore with the rest. You can bring me my meal any time."

The man returned in two minutes with a steaming platter of Mulligan Stew, crusty white bread and butter. Gid could hardly believe his eyes.

"Yes, sar," Hercules chuckled. "I go ashore like you say, but I buy me some food in de market."

Gid tasted the stew. It was fresh beef, onions and potatoes in good brown gravy. He laughed when he thought what Aaron would say if he knew about this excellent fare. When he had eaten his fill he counted out half the money in his pocket and gave it to Hercules.

"I haven't much cash," he told him, "so make this last as long as you can. We'll be here a week, maybe. Think you can find a job ashore till your leave's up?"

The cook's face fell. "Yes, sar," he answered. "But I hoped I stay with you."

"Well," said Gid, "I don't—er—we can talk about it later."

In the days that followed, Hercules turned out to be a continual surprise. He not only cooked delicious meals but cleaned the cabin faithfully, pressed Gid's uniform and stood watch when the young skipper went ashore.

In the course of the week Gid made several such expeditions. On one of them he posted a long letter to Mistress

Drake's Female Seminary, telling Peggy about the voyage from the Bahamas. He also paid a call at the Clarkson house. It distressed him to find Sam's mother looking so pale and quiet. She was very glad to see her son's friend, however, and he did his best to cheer her.

They had had one letter from the young prisoner. He was held in the hulks in Wallabout Bay with some hundreds of other Yankee sailors. It was very cold, he said, and their rations were poor and scanty.

The Clarksons had immediately sent off a large package of food and warm clothes, but they had no assurance it was ever delivered. In those days there were too many greedy hands helping themselves all along the line.

The brig and her cargo were finally put up for sale on March 12th. A big crew of stevedores had been unloading the casks of wine from the hold for several days, and word of its quality had spread through the city. Elegantly dressed merchants by the score were on the wharf when the bidding began.

Gid heard a single pipe of Madeira go for more than three hundred dollars and knew the Congress and the *Saratoga's* crew would reap a good profit when the money was shared out. Later in the day he had cause to be glad of the work Aaron and he had done on the brig itself. The sale price was at least a thousand dollars above the going rate, simply because the vessel looked so trim and tidy.

He took his belongings ashore, said good-bye to Francis Lewis and spent the night at an inn. Next day he went to board the coach for Egg Harbor. He had his foot on the step to climb into the vehicle when he heard a pleading voice behind him.

"Please, Captain, sar," said Hercules. "You let me come with you?"

Gid counted his few remaining paper dollars. There was just enough money to get him to Batsto with a dollar left over. He was wondering how to tell the devoted little cook that he couldn't go, but Hercules fished some silver coins from his pocket.

"I am me own mahn," he said stoutly. "Got English shillings, an' pay me own way."

He swung himself up to sit in the boot, on top of the luggage, and grinned at Gid so disarmingly that the boy gave in.

By the time he reached home, only a little over two weeks of his leave remained. It was a restless period for Gid. He roamed the marsh and woodland, warmed now by the sun of early spring. Skunk cabbage and jack-in-the-pulpit thrust leafy heads out of the brown mulch, and birds were singing everywhere. He heard cardinals and catbirds, song sparrows and white-throats and the quarrelsome bluejays. Once or twice he rode down the river to see Aaron. At other times he helped around the forge or the foundry, though work seemed to be slack just then.

Hercules, meanwhile, had made himself so useful that Mrs. Jones sometimes wondered how she had got along without him. He cut wood, washed clothes and ran errands for her, and was soon looked upon as a member of the household. Gradually they learned a bit of his history. He had been a servant in the home of a rich Englishman in Antigua. Before the gentleman died he had set Hercules free, but there was little chance for a free Negro to support himself on shore. So he had shipped as cook aboard a merchantman.

Early on March 29th, Aaron came up to Batsto and the two young men started the return journey to Philadelphia. Hercules offered to go with them, but as he had never signed on as a Navy regular they told him to stay with the elder Joneses.

Both boys were anxious to get back to their ship. They could count on plenty of action under the dashing John Young, and they wanted to hear the yarns of their friends about the port of Cap François. Crossing the Delaware on the ferry, they looked eagerly up and down the river, but the trim masts and spars of the *Saratoga* were nowhere to be seen.

They took a small room together at an inn and went to call upon Francis Lewis. The commissioner greeted them in friendly fashion but could give them no news of the sloop-of-war.

"She must have been delayed longer than Young expected at Cap François," he told them. "Or possibly she's been taking more prizes on the way north. But she'll get here, never fear."

"What should we do then, sir?" Gid asked. "You see, it's a bit expensive staying at the inn, and we've had no pay for some time."

Lewis pursed his lips. "That does make it hard," he agreed, "but there's no money in the treasury. What we realized on the sale of your brig went to pay back debts. Of course there'll be prize money, but it can't be shared till the *Saratoga* reaches port."

That was the first of several meetings with the commissioner. The boys waited with what patience they could. Aaron prowled about the waterfront, rounding up the members of the prize crew, while Gid explored out-of-the-way parts of the city. He was especially interested in the ironmongers' shops. He knew something about iron and the prices charged for ornamental iron pieces amazed him. Often the castings were crude and the quality of the iron itself was far below the Batsto standard.

They hung around the city for three weeks and more, until the money they had brought from home was nearly gone. There was news in plenty from other ships. A big fleet of Yankee merchantmen had set sail from Havana in mid-March, escorted by the *Confederacy*, the *Deane* and the privateer *Fair American*. The first of them came up to Philadelphia on April 17th, reporting that the convoy had been attacked and scattered by raiders. The frigate *Confederacy*, commanded by Captain Harding, was captured. However, a few days later the *Fair American*, with young Stephen Decatur in command, led nearly twenty merchant ships into the Delaware.

Surely, Gid thought, some of these vessels would have word of Captain Young's whereabouts. But while several skippers reported seeing the *Saratoga* at Cap François, none of them knew where she had gone afterwards.

At last Francis Lewis agreed that there was no point in keeping the two young officers in Philadelphia. He promised to let them know by the first post if their ship turned up.

By this time most of their crew had drifted off, joining the privateers and letter-of-marque ships that lay in the harbor. Aaron himself was offered a second mate's berth in the *Fair American* and took it with the blessing of the Board of Admiralty. So Gid was left to journey home alone.

He had time to do some thinking in the coach. Hard as he tried to resist it, he could no longer escape the feeling that the *Saratoga* had been captured or sunk at sea. If she did come home safely at last he would be more than delighted. But in the meantime he couldn't be expected to wait around at loose ends.

In his mind an idea had been forming. Almost as soon as he reached home, he talked to his father about it, and that evening he went to see Colonel Cox.

The proprietor of the ironworks welcomed him warmly. "I've heard great things about you, young man," he said. "But I thought you'd be at sea again by now. Aren't you still sailing under John Young?"

"I wish I were, sir. I'm still in the Navy, but right now I seem to be a midshipman without a ship. Captain Young hasn't been heard from in six weeks and he's nearly a month overdue in Philadelphia. So all I can do is stand by. I'd like to earn my keep while I'm waiting, and that's what I came to see you about, sir."

The colonel nodded slowly. "Of course," he said, "you can have your old job back at the works, though things are a bit slow now. We get fewer orders from the Congress because of lack of funds. So our tonnage is down."

"Yes, sir," Gid answered eagerly. "But there's less profit

in plain tonnage than there is in quality ironware. We've got the purest iron anywhere around, and we've got good molders and foundrymen. What I'd like to do, if you'll let me, is try some fancy castings. I saw a lot of them in the city, selling at high prices and selling fast."

"Hmm," said the colonel, and rubbed his chin. "Sounds as if it might have possibilities. But where would you get your designs for the patterns?"

Gid gulped. "I'd make 'em myself, sir. Anyway I'd like to try it. I've got some ideas and I know how to handle wood."

Cox bounced to his feet and slapped the boy on the back. "Good!" he exclaimed. "Let's see what you can do!"

With that encouragement the boy set to work at once. He had a fair assortment of tools—planes, chisels, gouges and veiners—and there were pieces of basswood and bull pine in the shed at his home.

The first thing he tried was a simple fireback with a fluted border, carved with great care. When the wooden model was done he was far from satisfied with his workmanship, but he felt the piece was in better taste than some of the more ornate things he had seen in Philadelphia. He carried it over to the foundry and gave it to the head molder.

Gid's next attempt was a smaller but more difficult job —a trivet with a filigree design of interlacing ivy leaves. It took him a week of painstaking work but he was proud of the finished pattern.

When he took it to the foundry he was surprised to see

a row of black iron firebacks, cast from his first design. His father was there, looking them over.

"I told 'em to try a dozen o' these," he told the boy. "They look pretty good, and the colonel thinks we should send 'em up to the city to see if there's a market for 'em."

"I'd rather you didn't," said Gid. "I can do a lot better, an' I'd like anything we sell to be good enough to carry the Batsto mark. That way we might get a reputation. Now this trivet is more like what I mean."

He held out the graceful carving and his father whistled in surprise.

"Why, son, that's really pretty!" he exclaimed. "It'll take some careful casting but I reckon we can do it."

In the weeks that followed, Gid felt he was making real progress. The work was hard and he was often disappointed, but he had begun to know something of the joy that comes to a creative artist. He fashioned andirons, hearth baskets and hitching posts. Once he copied the head of his mare Blossom as a model for the top of a post.

Then he tried another fireback. This time he took Anthony Castoff's drawing of the *Saratoga* and carved it faithfully in low relief on the broad, flat surface. When it was finished he proudly cut the Batsto mark in the lower corner—the first time he had been willing to sign his product.

Some of Gid's designs had already been shipped to Philadelphia and had commanded a ready market. Colonel Cox was more than pleased by the addition to his business and insisted on paying the boy an increased share of the profits.

"Pound for pound," he said, "these things bring five times the price of cannon balls or iron pipe. So just keep at it, my lad. You're worth all we're paying you."

For two months there was no word from the Board of Admiralty. Finally, in June, Gid packed his saddlebags, mounted his mare and rode northward. This time he had plenty of money in his pocket, the sun was warm and the fields green. There was every reason for the boy to be happy. But he couldn't seem to enjoy himself as long as the *Saratoga's* fate remained uncertain.

He put up at the Bull and Stars that night, left the mare at the inn stable and crossed by the ferry in the morning. Francis Lewis was deep in work at the office on Front Street, but he remembered Gid and urged him to sit down.

"I fear there's little to tell you about your ship," he said. "The Tory papers in New York have had her captured at least twice, and the last time they reported Captain Young was killed. But since they're sure to be wrong in two cases out of three, we haven't yet given up hope."

Gid found little comfort in those words. "Where would you say that leaves me, sir?" he asked.

The commissioner held up his hands. "We can hardly post you to another ship," he said. "The Navy has few of them left. Of course there are privateers like the *Holker* and the *Fair American* in port, but they've been so successful that young officers are standing in line to get aboard them. I think you'd better resign yourself to remaining on the inactive list. Of course," he added wryly, "without pay."

Gid smiled. "That doesn't bother me. It's not knowing what's become of my friends. If there's any real news I hope you'll let me know."

He took his leave and went down to the docks. If the *Fair American* was in harbor he might run into Aaron. Shortly he met one of the old hands from the *Douglass's* prize crew coming out of a waterside tavern. Yes, the seaman told him, Mr. Mathis had come in from a voyage. But when Captain Decatur had taken command of a bigger privateer, the young mate had gone with him. They had put to sea a few days before.

Gid wandered up High Street to a large shop where ironware was sold. A couple of fashionably dressed ladies came in while he was there and he was pleased to hear them admiring some of his work.

"I *must* have that pair of fire-dogs," said one. "They're new and different—so artistic, too. Sally Otis will simply *die* of envy when she comes to tea next week!"

*   *   *

There was one thing he could do to relieve his loneliness, he thought. Lying in his bed at the Bull and Stars that night, he resolved to start for Burlington at sun-up. It was only a twenty-mile ride and he could be there well before noon.

He hadn't heard from Peggy Lane for more than two months. It was a year since they had seen each other, and then only for an hour. The farther he rode, that bright June morning, the less confident he became. Once, after crossing the Rancocas Creek, he almost turned the mare's

head homeward, but a stubborn streak helped him overcome his shyness.

Mistress Drake's Seminary was a forbidding stone mansion set among trees. There was a wall around the place
and a dour-faced Scotch caretaker stopped Gid at the gate.

"No gentlemen are allowed inside," he growled. "'Tis
one o' the rules. Besides, the young ladies are leavin' today
for the summer holidays."

Gid didn't know what answer to make but at that moment he looked up at the house and saw blonde curls
at a second-floor window. The girl's face disappeared before he could be sure, but he became suddenly bold.

"Thank you," he told the gatekeeper. "I came to escort
one of them when she leaves." And smiling he settled
back in the saddle to wait.

In three or four minutes the door of the mansion opened.
There was laughter and an excited chatter of voices. Then
Peggy left the others and came tripping down the walk.
She was dressed in yellow, with a wide-brimmed leghorn
hat, and had a light traveling cloak thrown over her arm.

As she approached the gate she nodded demurely at the
Scotsman, then threw Gid a mischievous glance. "So good
of you to come, Mr. Jones," she said. "The coach will be
here directly. By the way, Angus, you might fetch my bag."

The gatekeeper limped off toward the house and Gid
dismounted in haste. She put out both her hands to him.
"Oh!" she breathed. "It's good to see you, Gideon!"

He had no words to answer, but words didn't seem to
be needed just then. By the time the coach drove up and
the other girls joined them, they were talking naturally.

He helped them in and rode beside the carriage to the wharf, where a sailing packet waited to take them down to Philadelphia. When he headed southward he had Peggy's promise that she would be coming to Batsto for a visit the following week.

THE YOUNG LADY stayed at her uncle's house until early in July, and before she left Gid knew she was the one girl he wanted to marry. On her part Peggy felt the same way. But, as Gid's parents pointed out, they were both very young, and so they agreed to wait until the war was over.

Because he now had a definite goal in sight, the boy worked harder than ever at his iron molding that summer. The new Batsto designs were in high favor, not only in Philadelphia but in many New Jersey communities. The ironworks were showing a handsome profit and Gid's fortunes flourished accordingly.

The frosty days of fall came, and in late November the boy received a letter from Aaron Mathis. Briefly it mentioned a good voyage and prizes taken, informed him that Aaron was in good health and asked him if he could be at the office of Robert Morris, the Agent of Marine, on December the fourth.

Wondering what it was all about, Gid made preparations for the journey and rode north on the third. He found the citizens of Philadelphia looked on the outcome of the war more confidently since the surrender of Lord Cornwallis at Yorktown. True, the British still held New York, but their commanders seemed to have lost heart for the conflict. There were even predictions that peace might come within another year.

The first face Gid saw when he entered the Morris office was that of Nat Penfield. With a whoop of pleasure he embraced his old shipmate, then turned to Aaron, who stood grinning nearby.

"No wonder you wanted me here," he told the Mullica River boy. "The *Saratoga* must be home—is that it?"

Aaron's face changed. "No," he said, looking at the floor. "You'd better hear it from Nat."

At that moment Robert Morris came in. He was introduced to Gid and got down to business at once.

"Here's the accounting of wages due each of you for service in the *Saratoga*," he said, passing out slips of paper. "Look them over, please, and sign the receipts."

Puzzled still, Gid checked the dates and the amount. Not a very large sum but it appeared to be correct and he signed his name.

"Thank you, gentlemen," said the busy financier. "Here's the money. As far as the Continental Navy is concerned, you are all now on leave of absence."

They walked out into the crisp winter air. It was near noon and Nat suggested dinner. At a nearby tavern they took a table in a corner by the fire.

"Well," said Gid, looking at the sober faces of his friends, "let's have it."

Aaron cleared his throat. "First of all," he said, "Nat just got out o' prison a few days ago. That's why we didn't hear anything earlier."

"That's right," Nat nodded. "I was trying for the Delaware with a snow we took, somewhere off Nassau. That was the eighteenth o' March. About three weeks later, when I was nearly home, a pair o' British frigates ran me down. They took the snow to New York and sent us prisoners to York, in Virginia."

"But what about the *Saratoga?*" Gid asked.

"Let's see," said Nat. "You were with us when we captured the *Tonyn*, weren't you? Then came the *Douglass*, and you and Aaron sailed her home. Well, we took another ship, the *Diamond*, and went on down to Haiti. Quite a place—that Cap François. A dreamy, warm sort of town, with palm trees waving and a great black mountain up behind it. We were there for a month or more, and the whole harbor was full of American ships, mostly merchantmen.

"Captain Young was supposed to bring home the military stores that Carabasse was keeping for us. But we found some French admiral had helped himself and there wasn't much left. We had time for a lot of shore leave and everybody had a good time. Do you remember how Barent Sebring used to brag about his luck with women? Well, he got tangled up with some French mademoiselle and he'd have been in a duel if we hadn't hustled him back to the ship. It doesn't seem so funny, any more, though—"

His voice trailed off and his face grew sad as he continued.

"About the middle of March there was a big merchant convoy ready to sail north. The captains all went to a farewell party at the governor's house and in the morning we set out—thirty or forty sail of us. The *Saratoga* was helping guard the fleet. We were in the lead and well out to port on the eighteenth, sailing along off the Bahamas. That's a date I'm not likely to forget. It was blowing pretty hard then and kicking up a sea. About eight o'clock the lookout reported two sails to the westward.

"You know Cap'n Young. Wind or no wind, he ordered full canvas spread and away we went after 'em, heeling so far our scuppers were under half the time. By noon we were almost in cannon range, but the weather had got so bad the guns couldn't be aimed. We ran up alongside the first vessel—snow-rigged—and she struck her flag. Young didn't wait a second. He had the longboat lowered over the side and sent me with a prize crew to board the snow.

" 'Make sail and follow us,' he yelled at me through the wind. Then he went tearing along after the other ship. We got aboard our prize somehow and were just hoisting sail when there came a terrible gust of wind. It ripped away half our canvas and laid us on our beam ends. Honestly, I thought we were done for. When we righted I looked at the sea where the *Saratoga* had been—and—"

Gid stared at the other midshipman, wide-eyed. "Yes?" he whispered.

"She wasn't there any more," said Penfield huskily.

*   *   *

206

The war ground finally to a halt, and in the spring of 1783 Gid and Peggy Lane were married in Philadelphia's Old Christ Church. Aaron, now captain of his own merchant brig, stood up with Gid as best man. Sam Clarkson regained his freedom in time to be one of the ushers, along with Nat Penfield. And Nancy Breckinridge was Peggy's maid of honor.

The young couple took a modest brick house on Camac Street, for Gid had gone into business for himself in the city. He had a forge and foundry where he used good Batsto iron to make some of the most beautiful wrought and cast iron pieces of the period.

To the Camac Street house, on the eighteenth of March, 1786, came three men, all young and all prosperous looking. As they rapped at the knocker the door opened wide and a gray-haired little Negro grinned broadly at them.

"Mahster Sam—Mahster Aaron—Mahster Nat—come right in, gentlemen!"

"Thank you, Hercules," they said in chorus and handed him their greatcoats and three-cornered hats.

Gid and his pretty wife rose as the three were ushered into the parlor, and they chatted for a while until Hercules called them in to dinner. Then, around the table, they stood silent for a moment. There was a faraway look on Gid's face as he raised his glass.

"To a great ship—a gallant captain—and good friends," he said softly.

"The *Saratoga*," quiet voices answered. "May she rest in peace."

www.ingramcontent.com/pod-product-compliance
Lightning Source LLC
Chambersburg PA
CBHW060551190726
48283CB00003B/958